The Healer

Lorraine Shoong-Oy Gassner

Copyright © 2010 by Lorraine Shoong-Oy Gassner
First Edition – October 2010

ISBN
978-1-77067-204-8 (Hardcover)
978-1-77067-205-5 (Paperback)
978-1-77067-206-2 (eBook)

All rights reserved.

Though this story is inspired by real events, the characters are all composites and are not meant to represent any one individual.

No part of this publication may be reproduced in any form, or by any means, electronic or mechanical, including photocopying, recording, or any information browsing, storage, or retrieval system, without permission in writing from the publisher.

Published by:

FriesenPress

Suite 300 – 777 Fort Street
Victoria, BC, Canada V8W 1G9

www.friesenpress.com

For information on bulk orders contact:
info@friesenpress.com or fax 1-888-376-7026

Distributed to the trade by The Ingram Book Company

To Leslie

— Chapter One —

"The bastard!" she cried, slamming the door behind her. With quick, light footsteps, the titian haired beauty came into the main room of the rented house she shared with two friends. At four feet ten, Lorelei McMillan projected more energy and personality than many far taller people did. She was a striking figure no matter what she wore, but tonight she was especially so in her peacock-blue backless silk dress and matching stiletto-heeled shoes.

From a beanbag chair in the corner, a voice said, "Who?"

"That Alan…I had to tell him to piss off…the bastard," she repeated, as a tall figure stood up. Myles Curry, one of her roommates, cast her an amused glance before saying, "You're not in Australia anymore, Lorelei. Here we tell people to 'fuck off' when we're angry." He laughed as she tossed a cushion at him.

Green eyes flashing, she continued, "What else could I do? Here I am dressed to kill, and he tries to handle the goods as soon as I get in the car. It was supposed to be a date, not a bloody mauling! And I'm starving; he couldn't even feed me first before he tried it on." She went into the kitchen, her heels click-clicking on the linoleum. Myles followed.

"Maybe he thought you'd be an easy conquest…you do go out with a lot of guys," he said, somewhat tentatively. Lorelei's temper could flare quickly, and she was already in a fighting mood.

She stopped rummaging in the refrigerator to protest, "That doesn't mean I'm bonking them all," she said.

"Only most of them?" Myles teased.

"Well, yeah, 'most' is different from 'all' isn't it? And what are you doing home anyway? I thought you were going out tonight? And where's Paula?"

Lorelei was very adept at directing the conversation away from herself whenever she felt uncomfortable with the direction it was taking. She did not like her actions to be scrutinized too closely, not even by her closest friends, and she saw no reason to do any self-reflection. At twenty-six, she was a few years older than most of her student contemporaries at Pacific University in the sleepy west coast town of Tillicum. She had entered the Fine Art program a year after her separation from her husband, and it had been a godsend. Now, in the spring of 1978 she felt at ease with her fellow art students, who shared her quirky sense of humour and her drive to create.

Though she had been fond of David Garrison, he was very staid and conservative, being a successful businessman. He had offered her financial stability and a certain social cachet, but she had been bored beyond reason with the endless round of dinner parties and country club soirees. And David had been rather controlling, afraid as he was of her sassy, creative streak. In the end, she had taken to being as outrageous as possible in order to show him she wanted out. He had become very bitter, and had responded by making the separation tedious. The divorce proceedings ran as an undercurrent to her present life; her close friends could always tell when she had had a meeting with her lawyer. The telltale desire to get very drunk was always a giveaway. And there was something else lurking in her subconscious, something she could not yet name. Lorelei welcomed the distraction of a date gone wrong. She found some pizza in the refrigerator and helped herself to a slice, popping it in the toaster oven. While it heated, she asked Myles again, "Why haven't you gone out?"

He took a can of soda from the refrigerator as he answered, "Katy got sick and had to cancel. And I don't know where Paula is." Their other roommate was seldom home.

"You and Katy are the 'real thing' aren't you?"

A wide smile lit his pleasant face, framed as it was by dishwater-blond hair and wire-rimmed glasses that gave him a bookish look. He was obviously very much in love.

"Yeah, looks like it," he answered.

"What about that Mei girl you were hanging around with last year? I thought you had the hots for her?" Lorelei liked Mei Lundgren, but regarded her as too attractive to really befriend.

"Well, yeah, I did, but she's not interested. She had a bad bust-up with someone and is kind of gun-shy."

"Poor thing. Men are pigs! Present company excluded, of course."

"Always!"

Myles, a photojournalism student, was the sort that liked women as people, as opposed to sex objects, and enjoyed the company of many women friends. His less enlightened, envious male friends assumed he must have a "line" to attract so many women.

"Katy seems right for you," she said, and she's not as pretty as me, she thought. It didn't matter that she had no romantic interest in Myles; her ego demanded that she be one of the most if not *the* most, attractive woman in his circle.

"So are you just going to stay in tonight?"

"Yeah, don't feel like doing much else since Katy couldn't come out. Guess I'll just watch the tube. There must be a game on."

Myles settled in front of the television while Lorelei pondered what to do. She felt restless; she had expected to be out late and now, here she was, home on a Friday night. On a whim, she picked up the phone and called her friend Cathi-Ann McVie, who lived with her boyfriend Steve Harding, who was a non-social loner who preferred to be out fishing to anything else. She held the receiver some six inches from her ear as she had learned that Cathi-Ann had a tendency to speak several decibels louder than was necessary.

"Hey, Lore, what're you doing home tonight?"

"I might ask you the same thing."

"Steve didn't want to go anywhere. You know how he doesn't like people. What's going on? You got a plan?"

Lorelei told her. "I feel like getting legless."

"D'you want to go to the Palace Hotel?"

"Isn't that a biker bar?"

"Yeah, but they have a good dance floor and the Michael Allison Band is playing."

"Ohhh, he's dishy. I heard they are playing on campus next week." The predator in her began to speculate. "Right, I'll take a cab and meet you there." She hung up and called for a taxi. While she waited for it to arrive, Lorelei checked her hair and makeup in the hall mirror. She liked to be fully armed before she went into battle. A few minutes later, a car honking outside signalled the arrival of the cab; she grabbed her purse, and with a cheery, "Don't wait up for me!" to her roommate, she was out the door.

Fifteen minutes later, the car pulled up in front of a four-storey, frontier-style building. The hotel had been one of the original businesses of Tillicum a hundred or so years ago, serving the miners who had flocked to the area in search of a better life. Rumour had it that the hotel had also functioned as a bordello at that time. Whatever it had been, the hotel was still in business serving those whose idea of a good time included liquor, questionable interludes with the opposite sex, and loud music.

As she got out of the taxi, she could see Cathi-Ann getting out of another cab across the street; she waved as she came toward Lorelei. Of medium height and stocky build, Cathi-Ann projected a no-nonsense air. This, coupled with her tendency toward blunt, tell-it-like-it-is commentary made few want to challenge her. Tonight, she wore a flowing Mexican-print skirt topped with a white peasant blouse; her cloud of black curly hair and piercing gray eyes set off a face that was handsome rather than pretty. She, too, was a visual arts student at Pacific University.

"Well, Lore, I hope that there are some big, huffly guys here tonight," Cathi-Ann said as they stood in line behind a few other people. They could hear the band tuning their instruments as they waited.

"What about Steve?" asked Lorelei, knowing what the answer would be.

"Steve who?" replied her friend, an evil grin on her face.

Lorelei chuckled as they were admitted, thinking how shocked David and his stodgy colleagues would be if they could see what she was doing now, and whom she had chosen for friends. None of them would know fun if it hit them on the head.

As they entered the bar, the band began to play a pulsating rhythm that evoked ancient tribal rights of courtship. The place was fairly full, considering it was still early in the evening. With the darkness, the crowd, and the flashing strobe lights of the dance floor, it took a few moments to get their bearings. Spying a small available table off to the side, Lorelei led her friend to it.

They quickly ordered drinks, doubles of course, for both young women liked to get 'loosened up' as they put it, as quickly as possible, and it helped Lorelei to forget things she would rather not think about. She surveyed the crowd. Yes, there were several likelies present. And the band's lead singer was certainly sexy, though she was always a little suspicious of a man who was that pretty. She liked the idea of all the men in the room having eyes only for her, that she was so beautiful that gay or bisexual men would forget their predilections as soon as they set eyes on her.

Cathi-Ann pointed towards one man who was dark and well-muscled, and dressed in jeans and a black leather vest over an otherwise bare torso. With his long black hair and mustache, he was exactly the opposite of David, who had always sported a well-groomed collegiate look.

Their first drinks finished, a second round was ordered; a few minutes later the waiter came back with two drinks for each of them, and indicated the dark man standing at the bar. The man tipped his glass at them, before downing his drink. A shiver of anticipation went up Lorelei's back as she realized that he was coming over to their table. She gulped her drink down as she glanced at Cathi-Ann, and was chagrined to see that her friend was interested in him, too. Well, there were plenty of others here; let him make the choice. Fortunately, the band chose that moment to take a five-minute break. The man introduced himself as Blackie, and pulled a chair up to the table.

"So, what are a couple of foxes like you two looking for tonight? Some action?" he asked, showing a mouthful of gold as he grinned lasciviously at them.

"How do you know we're looking for action? We could be gay," said Cathi-Ann.

"Naw!" he guffawed. "You don't look like lesbians!"

"How do lesbians look?" asked Lorelei, gulping down her third drink. She felt alert and electrified, as she always did when she drank.

"Not like you!" he exclaimed, giving her the once-over look.

His choice obvious, Cathi-Ann said, "I see someone I know over there; I'll leave you two alone." She got up and went towards the other side of the bar. Just then the band returned and began to play a song that Lorelei had heard before; it started slowly, but turned into a hard-driving number that lasted five minutes or more. Blackie pointed towards the dance floor; she nodded, and they both downed the last of their drinks before leaving the table. The band was still playing a slow, sultry rhythm as Blackie took her in his arms and rubbed his crotch suggestively against her. She was relieved when the music segued into a primal beat; Blackie released her and they began to gyrate separately to the music. Though she had no intention of sleeping with him, she wanted him to think the possibility was there as she flirted with her eyes. The song lasted longer than expected, a good ten minutes or more, until after a lengthy crescendo, it suddenly ended.

Lorelei, who had been dancing with her eyes closed for a few seconds, looked up. Blackie was nowhere to be seen. Suddenly, she staggered as someone shoved her hard in the middle of her back. She whirled to see a tall, thin, bleached blonde woman with a pinched face and far too much mascara standing there, hands on hips, glaring at her.

Not in the least intimidated, Lorelei exclaimed, "Hey, watch it!"

The other woman shoved her again, this time in the chest, as the other people on the dance floor began to back away. Lorelei shoved the woman back.

The blonde pushed her again, nearly knocking her off her high heeled shoes, as she shrieked, "Bitch! No one dances with *my* man and gets away with it!"

"And no one calls *me* 'bitch'!" cried Lorelei as they two women launched themselves at each other. She didn't have the taller woman's reach, but a childhood spent on an isolated sheep station in Australia had given her a strength few would have believed she had. The other woman reached for Lorelei's hair, smiling malevolently as she grabbed a handful and yanked hard. The smile did not last long as Lorelei elbowed her in the stomach, and, as the woman doubled over in pain, Lorelei grabbed her left arm and yanked up behind the other woman's back and kicked at the back of her knees. The blonde went down, cursing loudly. From out of nowhere, Cathi-Ann leapt to Lorelei's aid, and as the three woman rolled around on the floor, several large, black-clad bouncers took hold of Lorelei and Cathi-Ann and dragged them both, kicking and screaming, to an exit door, and threw them out into the alley beyond.

– Chapter Two –

Groaning softly, Lorelei slowly came to semi-consciousness. She was dead, she had to be. No living person could survive the pain in her head. Her body protested painfully as she tried to shift position slightly; dim memories of the fracas in the bar the night before drifted into her awareness. She was very thirsty and there was a moldy taste in her mouth.

No, she was not dead, not if she could feel this horrible, though she was reluctant to open her eyes as she did not know where she was. A full-to-bursting bladder screamed for her attention. Cautiously, Lorelei cracked one eyelid open, and was relieved to see that she was in her own room, but the perspective was odd. Opening both eyes, she realized that she could see under the bed which could only mean that she was on the floor.

She groaned again as she shifted position, fighting nausea as the room seemed to swirl around her. With an effort borne of necessity she heaved herself to her feet, nearly falling as the floor seemed to undulate beneath her as she clung to the dresser for support. Shivering, Lorelei realized that she wore only her bra and a half slip; somehow she had managed to remove her dress and panty hose before she had passed out.

A snoring sound that emanated from under the pile of blankets on the bed startled her. Whoever it was slept completely covered under the pillows and bedclothes. Had she brought a man home? It wouldn't be the first time she couldn't remember doing so. She sighed with relief as the body shifted and a small foot with lacquered toenails appeared; Cathi-Ann had obviously come home with her.

Still a little unsteady, Lorelei wrapped a tattered chenille robe around her body and went across the hall, where the old house's single bathroom was located. After answering nature's call, she splashed cold water on her face before daring to look in the mirror. The slightly greenish tinge to her cheeks contrasted sharply with her terra-cotta hair, which smelled of liquor and stale cigarette smoke, and hung in limp hanks about her face.

Her head pounding, she went to the kitchen praying that there was something cold to drink in the refrigerator. Finding a large pitcher of orange juice, she downed several glasses before her thirst had been slaked. Lorelei heard muffled noises coming from her bedroom; Cathi-Ann was stirring. A thud, followed by mumbled curses, preceded the sound of unsteady footsteps making their way to the bathroom. After what seemed an unusually long time, the bathroom door opened, revealing a much disheveled Cathi-Ann, who had obviously slept in her clothes. Eyes squinting against the morning sunlight that streamed through the dusty windows, she stumbled to a chair and carefully settled herself into it.

"Ohhh," she groaned dramatically as she propped her head in her hands. Exhaling loudly, she continued, "Don't blink so loud! I feel terrible. How did we get back?"

Lorelei sat in a chair opposite and passed her a glass of juice, which Cathi-Ann drank greedily. "A cab, I think," she replied. "Someone must have called one for us; neither of us was in a fit state. I suppose they don't throw women out every night."

"I dunno, it does get pretty wild in there," said her friend. As she tried to run her hands through her tangled hair, she winced. "Ow! What's going on? Lore, what's on the top of my head?"

Lorelei looked and was surprised to see a small cut. "You've hurt yourself somehow. It must have happened last night."

Cathi-Ann felt the wound. "*That's* where the blood on the pillow came from. I was wondering."

"What? You've bled all over my bed linens…laundry is the last thing I want to do."

"Well, it could have been worse, y'know. I bet those bouncers must have been really turned on by the sight of three women fighting."

"I don't know. I suppose they must see all sorts of things," replied Lorelei, not wanting to see the previous night's events as anything unusual.

Just then Myles came down from his attic bedroom. "Hey Myles," Cathi-Ann said. "Are you ever turned on by the sight of women fighting?"

"Oh yeah, all the time," the young man grinned, as he began to make coffee. "Why, what happened?"

They told him.

"Lorelei, something always happens when you go drinking! Like last time…"

"That was not my fault!" protested Lorelei. "I just ended up with the wrong fella!"

"Was that the guy who took you to Greenward Park and then tried to tear your clothes off?" asked Cathi-Ann.

"Yeah," said Lorelei, and then reminded her friends of the time when she had been drinking with other friends and ended up accepting an invitation for a late-night dinner from a man who was a friend of a friend. The problem was that she hadn't realized that she was the intended appetizer until the man had driven to the isolated part of the city park. Incensed, she had jumped out of his vehicle and walked all the way home in a cocktail dress and stiletto heels. "I dunno why I get all these jerks," she sighed.

Just then, the phone rang. Myles answered, spoke briefly, and then turned to them. "That was Katy, saying she had just ran into Steve; he was wondering where Cathi-Ann was."

"Well, I better go pretty soon," said Cathi-Ann. "When Steve has actually noticed I'm not there, it's time to go home."

"Hang on, I'll give you a ride in a bit; I'm going to go develop some photos. Hey, how was the Michael Allison Band last night? Did you even pay attention to them? They're playing on campus in a few days and I'm hoping to get an interview," said Myles. As a photo journalism student, he worked for the student newspaper.

"The singer was quite lickable, that much I noticed," Lorelei offered.

"Mmmm, hmmm," agreed Cathi-Ann.

"You predators! I'm glad Katy isn't like you two." The young man gulped the last of his coffee before continuing, "C'mon, C.A., let's go." Cathi-Ann dragged herself out of the chair and slowly followed Myles out the front door. After they had gone, Lorelei was left to her musings.

The house was very quiet, considering it was almost eleven in the morning. Only the occasional squeak of the eighty-year-old house settling could be heard. Lorelei had no idea if her other roommate, Paula Matson, was home, and she rather hoped she wasn't. A social work student, Paula projected the earnest desire to help that characterized members of her chosen profession. Lorelei certainly did not want to be helped; she would live her life the way she saw fit, however long it may be.

As for the men in her life, none of them had been worth keeping around for very long, which was just as well. The last thing she wanted was another boring, anal retentive David. Now that Blackie from last night, *he* might be worth tracking down again. The fact that he had a jealous and apparently dangerous girlfriend made him even more attractive. Lorelei stretched, bruised muscles protesting. Her back ached. She twisted from side to side as the back door, which led off the kitchen, opened. It was Paula.

"Oh, hi, Lore," she said, unloading an armload of books on to the table. "Oh, good, there's coffee." Lorelei watched as she made short work of pouring herself a cup. Being tall, and big-boned, she was in direct contrast to the petite Lorelei. With a chubby-cheeked face and wide hazel eyes, Paula projected the idealism that was the core of her personality.

"Where have you been?" asked Lorelei.

"It was my turn to do the overnight shift at the Crisis Line," replied Paula. "After I got off at nine, I went to the library for some books for an assignment."

"Oh." Lorelei could not for the life of her understand Paula's need to help people; at least she understood doing it as a paid job, but to volunteer at the hotline was just beyond her. If a people felt like jumping off a cliff, they should be allowed to do so. She stretched again, and winced as she did so.

All concern, Paula said, "What is it?"

The cynic in Lorelei wanted to brush off Paula's empathy as disingenuous, but she knew Paula well enough to know that she really did care, which was irritating sometimes, but not at the moment.

"Oh, my back. I must have done something to it last night." She described, in lurid detail, the previous evening's adventures.

"My God! One of these days you're really going to get hurt, and come to think of it, you've been complaining about your back a lot lately. Maybe you should see a doctor."

"No, no need for that, it's nothing," Lorelei hastily replied.

"Well, okay then. Maybe you could come with me to Kwok Lee's place later."

"Who's Kwok Lee when he's at home?"

"My friend who owns the health food store, the one that's trained in eastern medicine. I've talked about him before, remember?"

"No, not really." Paula's fervour for healthy living sometimes put a damper on Lorelei's ability to have a good time.

"So you'll come?"

"Yes! Alright!" she exclaimed, more to appease Paula than out of genuine interest. "But I'll need to have a bath and make myself human first."

A couple of hours later, after Lorelei had bathed and eaten, she felt much better. Once dressed, she admired her reflection in the hall mirror. In her tight jeans and low-cut emerald-green Indian blouse, with her thick, burnished-copper tresses falling about her shoulders, she could not fail to turn heads. A touch of eyeliner, a hint of green eyeshadow, and a dash of lip-gloss and she was ready. She looked up to see Paula watching her, an amused expression on her face.

"What?" Lorelei asked.

"You! Every outing is a production! We're only going downtown." Paula eschewed makeup except on very special occasions, and she paid little attention to fashion, preferring comfortable, loose clothing to the trends of the moment.

"Well, I must be prepared in case I meet anyone I wish to impress!"

"It's a lot of fuss and bother if you ask me. Let's get going." In a few moments, they were in Paula's ancient sedan, headed for Tillicum's downtown core. Lorelei was the only one of the three roommates who did not have a car. It was not that she could not drive; she was just reluctant to learn to drive on what was to her, the wrong side of the road.

Soon, they were walking along the main street of the picturesque seaside town. Fashionable young women shopping at the boutiques, long-haired leather-and-suede clad young men congregating outside the music store, young families waiting to get into the ice cream shop, and individuals scurrying along, packages in hand, made for an atmosphere of convivial energy on this sunny Saturday afternoon.

Lorelei always enjoyed people-watching, and was not paying much attention to where Paula was leading her. Her roommate had disappeared from view briefly before she realized that Paula had gone down Miner's Alley, a quaint, narrow walkway between two brick heritage buildings. She hurried to catch up. There she was, waiting in front of a door above which hung a sign painted with Chinese characters, with the words "Kwok Lee's Health Food and Vitamins" underneath. In the window there was a display of various bottles and jars of mysterious substances, as well as books and ornaments.

As they entered what appeared from the outside to be a small establishment, Lorelei pictured the proprietor; a small, wiry man with straight black hair and perhaps glasses, and a thick Chinese accent;

the stereotypical Asian male. Once she was inside, she realized that the store was actually very long and narrow. Both sides of the premises were lined with shelves stocked with ointments, vitamins, and the like, with one section given over to giftware. On the wall above the counter was a large poster depicting a dragon, golden toenails flashing; further down the same wall were smaller posters of bodily systems. The air was perfumed with the scent of sandalwood and fivespice. At the far end were refrigerators that held perishable goods, and a doorway with a beaded curtain, beyond which she could hear footsteps.

"Just one moment," said a deep male voice with a faint British accent. A few seconds later, a tall figure clad in black stepped through the obscuring beads. Lorelei did a double take as the man came closer. Surely this could not be Kwok Lee! He was over six feet tall, with skin the colour of honey, and long wavy dark brown hair. Large, slate-blue eyes were set in a high-cheekboned face, full lips, and a nose that was decidedly European. Of slim build, he moved as if he was acutely aware of every muscle. He was clad in what appeared to be traditional Chinese clothing; loose fitting black pants and a matching shirt with a Mandarin collar. On his feet he wore simple rattan sandals.

"Oh hello, Paula," he said, flashing a brief, brilliant smile. He was indeed a very handsome man. His eyes rested on Lorelei for a few seconds before he addressed Paula again. "What can I do for you?"

"That digestive problem I was having has gone away. At least I think it has."

"Come here; let's have a look at you." Paula stepped forward, and allowed the man to place the tips of his fingers at various points on her torso. Lorelei noticed that he seemed to be concentrating, as his eyes were shut. He exhaled loudly, and then opened his eyes.

"Mmm, yes, you've greatly improved, but you should continue the diet for another month, just to be sure."

"I was afraid you'd say that!" exclaimed Paula. "But I know that's the only way… I'll also take some more of those vitamins you recommended; oh, and my friend here is having problems with her back."

"The vitamins are on the rack behind you," he said. As Paula turned to look for what she needed, the man smiled again and said, "Kwok Lee Morgan at your service. And you are…"

Surprised at the name, she said, "Lorelei McMillan."

"Are you the Lorelei that lures men to their doom?"

This was not the first time she had been asked this question, but she had not been expecting it from this ethereal healer. Somewhat nonplussed, she replied, "I can be."

"I must be cautious, then," he said, solemnly. A few seconds ticked by, seconds that seemed very long, before he added, "It's not just your back, is it?"

"Oh, it's nothing, I just party too much sometimes, that's all."

"I could examine…"

"No! No, really, I'm fine!" she protested. He was very attractive, and ordinarily, she wouldn't think twice about having such a good-looking man touch her, but Kwok Lee frightened her, and she didn't know why.

Paula returned to the counter with her selections. After she had paid for them, she said, "Thanks, Kwok Lee, I'll let you know how it goes."

"Please do, and Lorelei, do come back when you're ready."

She said nothing as she went out the door, but could not stop herself from making eye contact with him just before the door shut behind them.

"Did he recommend anything for you?" asked Paula, as they made their way back to the car.

"I didn't ask."

"What? He could help you, you know."

"I'm not sure about that. Why did he touch you like that?"

"He can read the flow of energy in your body. That's how he diagnoses you."

"Oh, yes, and I have x-ray vision. Sounds like a nutter to me."

"Don't say that! You don't know him!"

"What's to know? He's just another lad on the make, though he's found a unique way of doing it."

As they got in the car, Paula said, "It's not like that at all! Open your mind, Lorelei. There are other ways of medicine than what's common here." On the way home, she explained that Kwok Lee had been born in Hong Kong of an Anglo-Chinese father who was a medical doctor, and a Chinese mother who had been a practitioner of traditional medicine. Apparently that side of his family had been involved in such things for many generations. Under his father's urgings, he had studied standard medicine for a few years in England, and then he had switched to Chinese medicine.

"Does he have a girlfriend?" asked Lorelei, as Paula parked the car in front of the house.

"No, actually, he says he's abstaining from women as sex interferes with his ability to concentrate on reading people."

Lorelei looked at her as if she had suddenly begun speaking in tongues. "What?" she asked, incredulous.

"It's part of his thing, his personal philosophy. He's trying to live as purely as possible, to be closer to the spiritual world."

"Hmph. Sure he's not gay?" That, to Lorelei, was the only reason a man would refuse sexual congress with women.

As they went into the house, Paula replied, "Lorelei! The world is not so black-and-white and superficial as you seem to believe. People are more complex than that. Personally, I think he's been very hurt somewhere along the way, and this is his way of protecting himself."

"If you say so," Lorelei grumpily replied. Having depleted what energy she could muster for the day, she was feeling exhausted. As Paula went to her room to sleep, Lorelei headed to her own bed. Damn! She had forgotten to change the sheets after Cathi-Ann had left bloodstains from her head wound. Swiftly, she changed the bed linens and then collapsed onto the bed and immediately fell into a deep sleep. Soon she was in a dream, a fearful dream in which she was being pursued by a strange red cloud, and just when it was going to engulf her, a gold-and-black dragon appeared and blew the cloud away. The dragon's breath smelled of sandalwood; with the exotic scent lingering in her senses, the images faded as she slept on.

— Chapter Three —

After a Sunday spent lounging about, Lorelei went to the university printmaking studio Monday morning feeling a little fatigued, but determined to face the busy week ahead. Since it was near the end of the semester, the art students were finishing the last of their works in preparation for the annual student art exhibit. Lorelei wanted to finish a series of etchings in time for the show. With scheduled classes over, students were free to use the studios to complete their projects.

As she entered the printmaking studio, she saw that several students were already there, including Cathi-Ann, who was busily grinding a slab of limestone in preparation for a lithograph. Lorelei went to the supplies cupboard and got the things she would need for her project, and cleared a space to work near her friend.

Cathi-Ann ceased working as she said, "I love lithos, but not this part, my arm gets tired, and you have to pay attention all the time so that you grind evenly."

Lorelei laughed as she replied, "That's why I prefer etchings and aquatints. Metal plates are easier to handle."

"Guess I love a challenge. You feel okay now after Friday?"

"Yeah, how about you?"

"I still feel like I went through the ringer; don't know why."

"Maybe it's the head injury," Lorelei chuckled, remembering their adventure.

"Ha, ha. Very funny. Every time I go out with you something

happens. Anything else happen over the weekend? Come across anyone likely?"

Applying tar-like liquid ground to a small, highly polished metal plate as she spoke, Lorelei recounted her meeting with Kwok Lee, but did not tell her how he had discomfited her.

"He sounds like just your flavour," said Cathi-Ann, wiggling her eyebrows at her.

"Mmm, hmmm. Well, I could certainly stand a couple of nights bonking him."

"Really, Lore," said Cathi-Ann, feigning shock. "My virgin ears."

Lorelei could not resist the obvious comeback, knowing as she did that it was no secret that Cathi-Ann possessed a strong libido. "That's the only part left, huh?"

Her friend exploded in peals of laughter. Nearby, Mike and Everett, two inexperienced young men, who had been trying not to look as if they were listening to every word of the conversation, tried valiantly to stifle their own laughter.

"Ha! Ha!" laughed Cathi-Ann. "Now you've got these guys going!"

"Not too hard to do, that," replied Lorelei, noticing that the space she had cleared to work was not big enough for her purposes. Everett was sitting at an otherwise unoccupied table with no work in front of him while watching Mike, who had moved to the area where silk-screening was done. Assuming that Everett was just there to socialize, she said, "I've no room here. Everett, I wonder if you could shift your manly buns so that I can use that table to work." The young, fair-haired man's face flushed bright red as he made room for her. Really, thought Lorelei, these virgins are no challenge at all.

The next few hours were given over to her work; first she inscribed her design on the ground-covered plate, and then immersed the plate in a bath of nitric acid solution in order to etch the design into the plate so that it could be printed. Once that was done, she removed the coating of ground with solvent and began the messy process of preparing the plate for printing. The ink had to be worked into the etched design with cheesecloth, and then the excess ink was carefully wiped away. Too much wiping, and the ink was removed from the lines; too little, and the design would not show. Once the plate was ready it was then run through the printer; Lorelei usually preferred the large, electrically driven printer to the smaller, hand driven one as the pressure was even, which almost guaranteed a successful print. She had "pulled" ten prints and signed and numbered them when her stomach began to rumble; her concentration had been so intense that she had been almost unaware of anyone else in the room as she worked. Now, she looked around her and noticed that Cathi-Ann was the only person other than herself present.

"Where is everyone?" she asked.

"Gone to see the concert. Remember, that band that we saw Friday night is here today," said Cathi-Ann, as she put away her work.

Lorelei scrubbed her hands with industrial cleanser as she replied, "Do you want to go out and watch? The singer is very doable."

"Uh-huh. Are you going to try for him?"

"Nah, but I always like to look, you know that."

Their cleanup finished, both young women made their way to the cafeteria where they bought wrapped sandwiches and fruit juice, which they took outside with them, where the band was tuning their equipment across the quadrangle. Several students were setting up folding chairs; still others were making themselves comfortable on the strips of grass between the walkways. Lorelei and Cathi-Ann opted to sit on the stairs that led to the library; this gave them a side view of the performers.

After the student body president had introduced them, the band began to play dark moody pieces and hard rock rhythms, with the occasional passionate ballad. Neither Lorelei nor her friend joined the girls who were wildly dancing in front of the band. The singer wasn't really her type, and though slightly suspicious of such pretty men as Michael Allison, under ordinary circumstances, Lorelei wouldn't think twice about making a play for him. For some reason, she just wasn't interested this time. Lorelei contented herself with watching the band and the crowd.

Some time later, as the band was taking a break, she noticed the singer sitting on a chair behind the stage area, a small knot of people congregating around him. She recognized Mei Lundgren coming from the concession, some twenty feet away from the rear of the stage. At that moment, the group of people around Michael Allison dispersed, and Lorelei got a clear view; the man's head tilted up as he made eye contact with Mei, but the young woman did not go toward him as Lorelei expected. Still, she had a feeling something would occur there. She had a sixth sense about such things.

The next week was spent in finishing her work and preparing for the student art exhibit. When the day arrived, Lorelei was not sure if she would attend the opening. Such gatherings were usually an eclectic mixture of young aspiring artists, their mentors, and the moneyed elite; if one wanted to make some headway in one's choice of career, some "schmoozing" was necessary. Usually, she was very good at such things, having honed her networking skills during her ill-fated marriage to David. Tonight, however, she just couldn't bear the thought of being trapped in a room with stuffed shirts and stringy, pearl-bedecked women, nor did she feel like attending the party that a young teaching assistant was hosting for the students.

On the afternoon before the art exhibition, Lorelei was buying a cup of coffee at the concession when she looked up to see Tomas Contreras approaching.

"Oh, hi, Tomas," she said. "How are you?"

"Fine, I guess." The dark-haired young man seemed dejected.

"You sure?"

He sighed. "Yeah, yeah." He paused. "You going to the thing at the gallery tonight?"

She told him she wasn't. "Why do you want to know?"

"I dunno," he shrugged. "I'm taking Mei to the party afterwards... I dunno," he repeated. "Never mind," he said, and walked away.

Well, that was strange, thought Lorelei as she drank her coffee. He almost seemed as if he was going to ask her out, yet he said he was going to the party with Mei. And he was presentable, if not very tall. Heading home, she wasn't sure what she wanted to do that evening, which was uncharacteristic for her. Usually she welcomed any opportunity to go out for the evening and here she was, absenting herself from the biggest event of the art department's year.

Once Lorelei was home, she found that her roommates were out. She decided to pamper herself. After a long, hot bubble bath, she gave her hair a hot oil treatment and did her nails. Lying on the couch, wrapped in her comfy chenille robe, and with cold cream smeared liberally on her face, she was watching an old movie on the television when the phone rang.

"Um, hi Lorelei, I know it's late, but..."

"Tomas?"

"Uh, yeah. I was wondering, it's probably too late, but have you eaten yet?"

"I had a little something a while ago... why?"

"Oh, well, I was thinking... you want to go to the Spaghetti House? My treat? No, probably not..." his voice drifted off.

"I thought you were going to the party tonight," she said.

"Well, I was there, but I left." He sounded sad.

Lorelei thought for a moment before she replied. He sounded so dejected. "Well, alright you're on, then. Just give me twenty minutes or so to get ready."

"Yeah, yeah, alright," Tomas answered, sounding a little brighter.

In short order, Lorelei was ready. She was sitting waiting for Tomas when Paula walked in. Seeing her fetchingly attired in an ultramarine blue velvet minidress with princess sleeves and a deep scoop neckline that emphasized her cleavage, Paula asked, "Is that what you wore to the opening?"

"I didn't go. I have a date," she replied.

"Who is your hapless victim, someone new?"

"No, not really. Just Tomas Contreras. You know him."

The smile faded from Paula's pleasant face as she said, "Y...yes, yes I do."

Seeing the look of concern in her roommate's eyes she said, "Paula, is there something I should know?"

"Well, he's been hung up on Mei for a long time, but she's not interested in him that way."

"Well, maybe he's ready to move on. Besides, it's only dinner, nothing more."

"Just make sure he knows that. If you have to let him down, do it gently, okay?"

"Always the social worker, aren't you? Don't worry, I'll be nice," she said, as a car pulled up in front of the house. "There he is. See you later."

Once in the car, Lorelei thanked Tomas for inviting her out for the evening.

"No problem," he said. He did not so much as glance at her, and said not a word more on the way to the downtown restaurant.

Oh great, thought Lorelei, I can see how this evening will go. Too late to change my mind now. She'd just have to make the best of it.

Lorelei's forebodings turned out to be accurate, for once they had ordered their meals, Tomas said, "You know Mei, don't you?"

"Not well, but yes," she replied.

"I know she likes me, but she says she doesn't want to be more than friends. She had a bad breakup with someone before; I just know I could help her forget him. It seems like every time I get close to her she shoves me away."

Wanting to be helpful, so she could at least say that the evening wasn't entirely wasted, she said, "Sometimes there just aren't any romantic feelings, Tomas, even though a girl may like you as a person."

"No! Not with Mei!" Tomas said, vehemently. "I know she likes me, she's just confused, that's all."

Try as she might, Lorelei could not get Tomas to talk about anything else all through the meal, a situation she found extremely tedious. When out on a date, even if she was not terribly interested in the man she was with, she liked to be the focus of the conversation.

It was one thing to touch on the topic of past disappointments, quite another to not allow for any other subject of conversation. She gave up on attempts at turning the conversation to herself, and merely supplied nods at intervals as Tomas droned on. After what seemed to be an interminable amount of time, they had finished their meals and Tomas had paid the bill.

Walking back to the car, which had been parked nearby behind the hotel where she and Cathi-Ann had had their adventure the Friday before, Lorelei paid little attention as Tomas continued to talk about Mei. She saw that there were very few people about. If she had been alone, she would have been nervous. As it was, she did not mind cutting through Miner's Alley on the way, since Tomas was with her. She noted that, though Kwok Lee's shop was closed, there was a light on inside.

Tomas did not start the car once they were seated in it. "Women. It's just not fair," he muttered.

"What's that?" Lorelei asked, startled. What was he talking about?

"Oh nothing." He leaned toward her, his hand on her bare knee. It had been a very warm late-April day, so she had eschewed pantyhose.

Shocked, Lorelei pulled back and said, "Wait a minute, Tomas…"

Suddenly he was on top of her; somehow he had let the seat down and she was on her back, unable to move. He was much heavier than she. His face inches from hers; she could see the glint of rage in his eyes. "You bitches are all alike! You all want it, but you have to play your stupid games!" He clamped his lips onto hers as he held her down with one arm while she felt his other hand move up her skirt. In vain she struggled against him, but her efforts only seemed to increase his determination. She heard the front of her dress rip before she felt his teeth on her left breast. Terrified and screaming she somehow managed to keep her wits as she wriggled her right knee into position and slammed it as hard as she could into his testicles. Howling with pain, Tomas twisted away from her, allowing her time to open the car door and escape. She ran blindly down the alley behind the hotel, losing her shoes in the process. There was not a soul to be seen. Lorelei went to the only place she thought she might get help. Oh God, she thought, as she banged on Kwok Lee's door. Let him still be here, please! She nearly screamed with relief as the door opened and she literally fell into Kwok Lee's arms.

"Lorelei? What has happened?" he asked.

Now that she was safe, she began to cry. She looked up at him, saw him avert his eyes from her exposed bosom. In a moment, he had taken off the ornate blue silk robe he wore and draped it around her.

"Stupid question. It's all too obvious what has happened. Come upstairs. I'll make you some ginger tea." Gently he guided her to the back of the store and up the narrow stairs to the apartment above. Even in her agitated state, she could not help but notice his bare, tightly-muscled torso and the narrowness of his hips beneath the jeans he wore, and the way his hair just brushed his shoulders.

He attended her carefully as she sat on a green velvet-covered settee; she pulled the robe tighter as she began to tremble.

"Why… am I shivering?" she asked, teeth chattering.

"It's the physical reaction to the trauma you've just suffered." He reached behind her and pulled a heavy, embroidered blanket around her. "Here, this will keep you warm while I make the tea."

She looked up at him, gratitude in her eyes as she whispered, "Thank you."

The settee she sat on was made of some sort of light-coloured carved wood, and the coffee table in front of her was made of the same wood, and inlaid in mother-of-pearl with a design of peonies and chrysanthemums. The walls were covered with seagrass wallpaper, and on the floor was a thick woollen carpet with an intricate geometric design. A large jade statue of a woman in classical Chinese dress stood in one corner; in the opposite corner a brightly-coloured ceramic Buddha sat on a side table. The atmosphere was one of quiet serenity.

Lorelei's eyes returned to the coffee table in front of her on which rested a rattan-framed hand mirror. Dreading what she would see, she raised it to her eyes. A lipstick- and mascara-smeared face stared back at her. Suddenly, she realized that her purse was still slung over one arm. She managed a faint chuckle. Here she was nearly raped, and she had hung on to her handbag. Finding tissues in the bag, she did the best she could to fix her face. As she did so, she heard the whistle of the kettle in the kitchen. In a few minutes, Kwok Lee returned, bearing a tray, which he set on the table in front of her. From a porcelain teapot decorated with a blue-etched dragon, he poured the tea into a matching handle-less, tulip-shaped cup and sat next to her.

"Wait just a moment; it's a little too hot right now. Would you like to tell me what happened? It usually helps to talk, and I'm ready to listen." His voice was gentle and kind, with no hint of impatience. Still, he was male, despite what Paula had said about his celibacy. Yet he had been very considerate so far. With nothing to lose, she told him about her evening with Tomas.

"I see," he said. Passing the teacup to her, he asked, "Does this happen often?"

She inhaled the ginger tea's spicy scent. Not having tasted the beverage before, she cautiously sipped it and found it to be delicious and said so.

"It is, and it will calm your nerves." He paused. "You don't have to answer my question if you're not comfortable doing so."

"No, Kwok Lee, I want to tell you. Yes, it seems to happen all the time. I don't know why, but many of my dates don't go so well."

"Maybe that's because in here," he said, pointing to his heart, "you really don't want them to."

"I don't know…" she said, doubtfully. "I was married to someone that everyone else reckoned was a 'catch' but he bored me immensely."

"And how did he feel about you?"

"When it was good, he found me exciting."

"Ah, you were yin to his yang, and you found difficulty finding that bit of yang that would have balanced you with him."

"I don't know…" she repeated.

"And something else; you *must* look after yourself. I sense part of your energy is struggling; your system is in danger of becoming over-balanced, and if that happens, you will be ill."

She sipped her tea as she thought. Lorelei did not know what to make of him. He seemed to be in tune with things she had no awareness of, and in other circumstances she would dismiss such things as bunk, yet somehow he was striking a chord deep within her. And he was so exotically handsome. She set her teacup on the table and said, "I'm so grateful, Kwok Lee, and I would be happy to show you how grateful… if you'd like." She stroked his thigh. Gently, he enclosed her small pink hand with his long-fingered, dusky one and removed it from his leg.

Still holding her hand, he said, "You offer yourself, but would be wrong for me to bed you, though I am very attracted to you." He poured more tea into her cup and handed to her.

When he had taken her hand in his, Lorelei had felt a slow heat deep inside her, which radiated to her extremities; a strange heat that was more than physical. She sipped her tea.

"Oh, this tea is making me hot," she said.

Kwok Lee smiled slightly as he answered, "It can do that." Looking into her eyes, he continued, "You need rest. Would you like me to take you home?

Suddenly, Lorelei felt exhausted as she thought about having to explain herself to her roommates. It was late, and she knew that Myles and his girlfriend, Katy, were probably home from the party, watching television. They would be all sympathy, and right now, that was the last thing she wanted. Looking into Kwok Lee's slate-blue eyes, fascinating eyes, really, with flecks of mahogany brown, eyes that seemed to hold all the wisdom of the east, she knew not what to say.

"You hesitate…going home is uncomfortable for you right now. You are welcome to sleep on the settee here. It's not very big," he smiled, "but then neither are you."

His voice sent a shiver down her spine. When he spoke to her, she felt as if there was no one else in the world, as if his awareness consisted only of her. "Oh, yes, I would like that," she said, knowing that there was no other answer she could have given. In short order, Kwok Lee had given her a pair of jade-green silk pajamas to wear; they were slightly large for her small frame, but set off her copper-red hair appealingly. While she was in the bathroom readying herself, he made the settee up as a bed for her. When she returned, the living room lights were off, and Kwok Lee was in the kitchen tidying up.

Acutely aware of wearing nothing beneath the thin pajamas, Lorelei crawled under the warm blankets and made herself comfortable. Kwok Lee stood in the kitchen doorway, silhouetted in the light beyond. She did not know if he had seen her cross the room; she looked at him, but his face was not discernable, silhouetted as he was in the light of the kitchen beyond.

"Lorelei, are you comfortable?"

She loved the way he said her name; as if his tongue tasted the very syllables. "Yes, I'm fine, thank you."

"Good. I'll bid you goodnight. Sleep well," he said, as he turned off the kitchen light. She heard him walk down the hall; and in a few seconds, the soft click of his bedroom door shutting.

Lying in the dark, Lorelei did not know what to think. He was obviously attracted to her. Was this celibacy thing for real? Was it just his way of playing hard to get? Or was Paula right, and he had retreated into celibacy as a sanctuary from a world of pain? She had never known such a man before. Most were like Tomas, ready to take advantage any time, if they weren't crushingly boring like David. If Tomas kept behaving the way he had with her, he surely would run into trouble someday. What would she tell her friends tomorrow? Despite her efforts to stay awake to think, her tired body won the struggle, and all thoughts of the morrow were lost as she sank into a deep, dreamless slumber.

– Chapter Four –

Next morning, after Kwok Lee had driven her home in his truck, Lorelei found Paula sitting at the kitchen table, drinking coffee. At her entrance, Paula looked up, startled at Lorelei's attire. Since her dress and shoes had been ruined, Kwok Lee had given her a pair of loose dark blue pants with a matching, long-sleeved top that had a mandarin collar and gold-coloured frog closures. Her feet were shod in simple black fabric slippers.

"Well, here's a story," her roommate dryly remarked. "What happened?"

Helping herself to a cup of coffee, Lorelei sat across from her roommate before she began to relate the events of the night before. "Oh, Paula, where do I start? If it wasn't for your mate Kwok Lee, I don't know what would have happened."

Alarmed, her friend said, "Why, what do you mean?"

"Tomas. I should have listened to you, Paula, he…" As Paula nodded, she continued, "He called last night, and he seemed sad so I felt sorry for him and I went out with him." She went on to tell her the complete story of how she had ended up at Kwok Lee's.

"He was so kind, Paula, and he doesn't even know me."

"That's what he's like, very caring."

"He can't be for real; there's got to be an angle somewhere," the cynic in Lorelei had surfaced, now that she was safe in her own home.

"No, that's the real Kwok Lee. He cares very much about other people, and in fact, I think he would make a better social worker than I do, he's far more intuitive than I could ever be."

"Yes…" Lorelei answered, her mind drifting to his admonishment to look after herself. That morning, he had awoken her with a fresh pot of tea that was, as he put it "good for cleansing" whatever that meant. She had refused his offer of food, to which he had replied that she had better eat as soon as she got home. Kwok Lee had been very solicitous, running her a hot bath into which he poured an herbal tincture that was supposed to help her focus her energies, and patiently waiting for her to be ready, not to mention the clothing he had given her.

On the way home, he had reminded her of what he had said about caring for herself, and had shaken her by asking if she had been having troubles with her womanly cycle. How on earth had he known that? It had been going on for months, but as there had been no undue pain associated with her menstrual problems, she had put it down to the stress associated with her divorce proceedings. She did not allude to any of this as she conversed with Paula.

"You should really report Tomas, you know, though it sounds like quite an adventure," said Paula, as Myles came in the back door.

"What does?" the young man asked as he helped himself to coffee. Leaning against the counter, he listened as Lorelei gave him an abbreviated version of the story she had just told Paula.

"My God!" he exclaimed, putting down his cup. "If I'd known…"

"What?" said the young women, in unison.

Myles told them that Mei and Tomas been together at the party, and it was evident that Tomas was territorial where Mei was concerned, even though she had been very clear that she regarded Tomas as a friend rather than a potential romantic partner.

"And Michael Allison was there!"

"Really?" asked Lorelei, intrigued.

"Yeah," said Myles. "And he seems to like Mei, and…" he paused.

"Go on! You men always say you don't gossip, but here you are, if this isn't gossip I don't know what it is," observed Lorelei.

"Amen to that," agreed Paula, smiling.

Myles cast the tall young woman an amused glance before continuing. Apparently, the musician's soon-to-be ex-wife had also been at the party. Though there had been a scene between her and one of the band members, no altercation had occurred between the woman and Mei, but it seemed that Mei had felt uncomfortable and had asked Tomas to drive her home.

"And Mei would not have accepted his advances; he went home angry and then asked me out," concluded Lorelei, sighing.

"Are you going to report him?" asked Paula.

"Why should I do that?"

"So that other women won't run the same risk."

"I don't think any other women will let him near them, once I get through telling everybody. That's the best deterrent, isn't it Myles?"

"Yeah, we men have nothing on you women that way; you've got that instant grapevine thing going. If all you gals decide that one of us guys isn't going to get a date, there's nothing he can do to change it."

The following week the campus was buzzing with rumours concerning the party, but Lorelei paid little attention to them. She did keep her ears open for further news of Tomas, but she heard nothing, nor did she see him. On Monday she heard from her divorce lawyer that David was continuing to make unreasonable demands regarding the disposal of their mutually-owned assets. Her first instinct was to tell him to let David have everything, for she had what she wanted, her freedom, but practically speaking, she needed the money. The stress was causing her to feel unwell. The ache in her back bothered her, and her digestive system was giving her some problems. And Kwok Lee had indeed been right; her monthly cycles were very heavy. She would be glad when she was officially divorced, and she could put her miserable marriage behind her.

That Friday, another student told Lorelei that she should go to the art gallery, where the student exhibition was proving popular, and she would be pleasantly surprised.

As she turned the corner toward the entrance to the gallery, Lorelei saw that someone was just leaving. She recognized Mei Lundgren, who with her exotic Eurasian looks, always turned heads, including hers. Lorelei swore secretly that if she were lesbian, Mei would be just the kind of woman she would go for.

"Oh, hello, Lorelei," she said, "I see you've sold quite a few of your prints; that's really good!"

Lorelei did not know the other girl well, but recognized her great talent in producing large, stirring oil paintings. And, of course, her fashion sense; no matter what she wore, Mei always seemed to have walked out of a magazine.

"And I sold a painting!"

Lorelei smiled, genuinely pleased for her. As they worked in different media, she felt no sense of artistic competition. "Which one?"

"The biggest one! *The Sea Goddess*!"

"That's great! Do you know who bought it?"

Mei flushed slightly. "Y...yes...Michael Allison...the singer."

Ah, thought Lorelei, I was right, there *is* something happening there. Aloud, she said, "Congratulations!" If she had indeed made a conquest of the very sexy Michael Allison, she had Lorelei's respect.

"Thank you! Hope you sell more prints; gotta go now!" Mei said, as she moved off.

"Right, see you later." As Lorelei turned to go into the gallery, she heard her name called.

"Oh, Paula!" she said as her roommate came toward her.

A little out of breath, the taller girl said, "I'm glad I caught you! Listen, are you interested in a job?"

"I've no choice, Paula. I haven't had that much from David yet."

"I know of a job that's going. Don't know if it's your thing, but it's working in a group home for people with mental health issues. It's pretty easy work; making meals, doing housework, and monitoring the residents."

"What do you mean, 'mental health issues'? Would I be babysitting crazy people?"

"Lorelei! Anybody can develop a mental illness, you know."

"Don't you need some kind of qualifications for that kind of work?"

"There's a certificate that you can get, but it's not necessary. Really, it just takes common sense and a little knowledge. You get a crash course before you start; and the money's not bad, union rates. Here, I'll write the name of the person you need to see at the Mental Health Office," she said, as she scrawled the information on a scrap of paper and handed it to Lorelei.

With nothing to lose, Lorelei decided to apply for the job. The money from the sale of her prints would not go far. The interview was straightforward; Lorelei had worked in a doctor's office at one point in her life, which seemed to work in her favour. After a one-day course in how to deal with individuals with a mental illness, she began to work in the small, three-bed facility.

The work was indeed uncomplicated, and Lorelei found, rather enjoyable. The residents could stay anywhere from two weeks to a year, and were most often, male. At present, there was only one, a young man named Carl Hanson, who had been a resident for only a week. Potential residents were screened by community nurses before being accepted in the home.

Carl, a tall, sandy-haired young man, had had sudden onset of his illness, which was not uncommon. He had confined his widowed mother in the basement of her home, and had been found running circles in the yard, naked, screaming obscenities. With the care he had received in the hospital, and the prescribed medications, he was on the way to finding stabilization. The only difficulty was that he was beginning to believe that he was cured, and therefore had no need of the medications. The house staff did not force residents to take their medications; instead, they simply recorded whether or not the medications were taken in the daily logbook, and passed the information along to the psychiatric nurses who visited daily.

Over the first two weeks of her job, Lorelei became comfortable with Carl. His pride and joy was his motorcycle, so she encouraged him to talk about it, even, on one occasion, bringing him a motorcycle magazine. One day, he said to her, "Are you allowed to go out with me?"

Startled, but sensing adventure, she said, "No one told me I couldn't."

"You want to go for a motorcycle ride up the coast? I gotta get out of here."

Lorelei looked at him; his eyes were much less dull than when he had first come into the home; that must mean he was much better, though it was sometimes difficult to convince him to take his medications.

"You're on, that sounds like fun." Privately, she wondered why she was consenting, as she wasn't a fan of motorcycle riding, but it was better than sitting and fretting about things. She wondered what her roommates would think. Deciding to play it safe in that regard, she arranged to meet Carl early next afternoon in front of a nearby coffee shop.

The next morning, Lorelei told Myles and Paula that she was going to run some errands and then perhaps go see Cathi-Ann that afternoon, which wasn't entirely a lie, as she really did have a few errands to run. As she approached the coffee shop, she could see Carl and his motorcycle in the parking lot. He was dressed in jeans and a leather jacket, and wore a yellow crash helmet. He barely said hello before he handed her a second helmet which she quickly strapped on. She was glad that she had worn her own brown suede jacket, though she had found it uncomfortably warm in the late April sunshine.

Carl started the engine, and she got on behind him, holding him around the waist. At first Lorelei was rather frightened, the air whooshing past her as the motorcycle sped along reminded her that, should they crash, there was nothing between her and the road. She held on very tightly until Carl shouted over his shoulder that she was squeezing him too hard. As she realized that he was keeping to the speed limits and not passing other vehicles recklessly, she relaxed and enjoyed the ride. Travelling this way was much different than going by car. Lorelei was very aware of the greasy smell of fast food restaurants as they left the city, and the scent of horses from the stables located just outside the city limits. They had gone perhaps twenty miles on the highway when Carl turned the motorcycle down a side road, which meandered through a pleasant rural neighbourhood; they passed several small hobby farms before reaching an area of dense forest. Then Carl turned off the road and parked the motorcycle behind a thick clump of bushes. Lorelei assumed that they were stopping to allow Carl to answer the call of nature, which he did, standing a discreet distance from her. When he was done, he said, "There's a nice trail down to the creek, here. An artist like you would like it." Well, he wasn't being exactly talkative, but he was thinking of her. "Why not?" she said. "I get inspiration from all sorts of things."

Lorelei followed Carl down the trail. A creek flowed beneath willow and maple trees, and though the sun was shining, the thick forest let almost no sunlight penetrate. Only very tiny patches of light could be seen peppering the forest floor like a spilled cache of golden coins. It was also very quiet; the occasional croak of a raven high above, and the burble of the creek being the only sounds Lorelei could hear. The artist in her was indeed inspired; so many shades of green; so many textures.

"It's pretty here, Carl," she said.

"Yeah, it's real nice," he answered.

Suddenly Lorelei felt very vulnerable. Here she was, alone in the forest with a man she did not know very well, a man who was just learning to cope with having a mental illness. Though he had no history of violence, Lorelei knew from bitter experience that any time she was alone with a man, she could be in danger. She had not forgotten about Tomas. What was she thinking, consenting to go on this jaunt with Carl?

"It's getting a little chilly," she said, hoping Carl would suggest going back to his motorcycle.

He made no reply and continued to puff on his cigarette. Lorelei noticed that there were several butts scattered about his feet. Carl finished his cigarette and threw the butt on the ground. Stamping it out, he began to mutter under his breath, and pace back and forth.

Alarmed, Lorelei said, "Carl, are you okay?"

"No, not true, not true," he muttered. "Got to...be safe...be clean." It was clear that he was becoming very agitated. He continued to ignore her.

"Carl? Maybe we should go." What was it that she had learned in the training session? Be calm; talk the person through the episode. "Come on, let's go back to the bike; you must be worried about leaving it." Lorelei appealed to the pride he had in his motorcycle, the only thing he owned. She began to lead the way back to the trail, hoping he would follow.

He seemed to heed her, as he began to walk behind her. Lorelei tried to walk quickly without looking like she was in a hurry. Had they really come such a long way? She became aware that Carl had stopped; turning around, she saw him standing very still, staring intently at her. He seemed to be undergoing some inner turmoil.

"Carl?"

He stared silently in her direction, his eyes unfocussed.

"Carl?" She was becoming very frightened.

Suddenly, he lifted one arm, and pointing at her, shouted, "You!"

Instinctively, Lorelei turned and ran; she could hear Carl close behind her. Though the road was so close that she could hear cars passing by, the trail was steep, and after a few minutes struggling with the slope she knew she had no hope of staying ahead of him. He was only three feet behind her when she dashed past him and began to run back toward the creek. He fell as he tried to lunge at her; this gave her some time to put some distance between them. Roaring, he pursued her, crashing through the woods like an angry moose.

Lorelei reached the creek, and not knowing what else to do, tried to gain the opposite bank, but being higher than she could easily climb, and muddy, she could not get over it. Blindly she ran down the creek, slipping and falling twice as she did so, and swallowing some water in the process. Still Carl came after her, calling her name as he ran.

She encountered a huge log lying across the forest floor, diverting the flow of the creek. Glancing over her shoulder, she could not see Carl, but she could hear him. Hurling herself over the log, she realized that there were several logs lying roughly parallel with each other. Lorelei knew she could not run much more, she would have to hide. She found a deep space between two of the logs, and squeezed herself into it. By chance, the space she had found allowed her to wriggle under one of them. Cringing as she encountered many-legged creatures in the slimy dampness, she wedged herself in as tightly as she could. Keeping stone-still, and her breaths shallow, she listened. Yes, that was Carl, splashing back and forth in the creek beyond, looking for her. He grunted loudly in frustration; through a chink under the log, she could just see him, standing not six feet away. Lorelei forced herself to remain calm, though her heart was pounding so loudly that she was afraid Carl would hear it. He was panting heavily, his eyes darting back and forth. Some sixth sense must have told him she was nearby, for he did not move for several minutes, after which he called,

"Lorelei! I didn't mean to scare you! Come back!"

She was too frightened to make a response. After a few more minutes, he seemed to make a decision, and began to move back the way he had come. After a very long time, Lorelei heard the motorcycle start and move off down the road. When the sound of its motor faded into the distance, she finally allowed herself to relax and climb out from under the log. The light was beginning to fade, if she did not get out of the forest soon, she would be there all night, which was dangerous, as she was beginning to shiver. Brushing dirt, dead leaves, and insects off her, she began the trek back up to the road, resolving to hitchhike home.

Once she had climbed up out of the forested gully, she began to walk towards Tillicum, turning and holding her thumb out as she heard cars approaching. The drivers would slow down as they approached and then speed up. I must look a fright, thought Lorelei as she trudged on. The sun was very low on the horizon when she heard a vehicle coming toward her; it was a truck, an old brown Ford that looked somehow familiar. Elation overcame her as she recognized the driver, who pulled over a short distance ahead of her. Kwok Lee! It was Kwok Lee!

– Chapter Five –

Trembling, Lorelei climbed into Kwok Lee's truck. Seeing her distress, he pulled further over to the side of the road, and turned the heat up. Alarm plain on his face, he exclaimed, "Lorelei! What has happened to you?"

Such gentle concern from others usually made Lorelei suspicious, but once she looked into Kwok Lee's worried eyes, all such cynical tendencies vanished. How could she not trust this considerate man who was so different from every other man she had known?

"Oh, Kwok Lee," she began, her teeth chattering, "it's so stupid of me…"

"Wait, you're hypothermic," he said. "If you do not get out of those wet clothes, you will be ill."

Slightly taken aback, Lorelei said, "What?" Maybe she couldn't trust him, after all; men often went to creative means to get her to take her clothes off, though most of the time, she was a very willing participant.

Noticing her hesitation, Kwok Lee continued, "I do not have an ulterior motive, Lorelei. Medically speaking, you will warm up faster if you remove those cold, wet clothes." He reached a long arm behind the seat of the truck and pulled out a soft, woolly blanket. "Here, wrap this around you while you get those wet things off."

She was shivering, despite the heater. Wrapping the blanket around her, she struggled to get out of her muddy, wet clothes while Kwok

Lee looked the other way. When she was done, she pulled the blanket tightly around herself. Kwok Lee reached behind the seat again and produced a thermos; opening it, he poured a cup of tea and handed it to her. The scent of jasmine filled the cabin of the vehicle as she drank it. In a few minutes, she felt the heat of the beverage warming her from within.

"Do you feel better?" Kwok Lee asked.

"Yes, yes, I do, thank you. I am warmer now," she replied. Looking out the window across the fields on that side of the road, she continued, "I can't believe that I've been so stupid…"

"Tell me," he said, softly.

Her eyes on her small, pale hands where they rested in her lap, Lorelei was unsure of what she feared she would see in his face. Empathy would reduce her to tears, while ridicule would provoke anger. Either way, she did not want to lose control of her emotions. She took a deep breath, and began to tell Kwok Lee about her afternoon with Carl. When she had finished, she cautiously turned to look at him.

He merely looked at her for a long moment before putting the truck into gear and pulling out on to the highway. They had travelled in silence for some minutes before he said, "Taking such risks makes you feel alive, but lately you've feared you will not be alive much longer. Am I right?"

Startled, Lorelei looked at him in amazement. She felt as if he could see into her very soul. "Yes…yes, you are," she said, "but how…"

"When I talk to people, I see little movies in my head about their lives. I can tune them out if I choose, but with you," he glanced at her, "I very much want to tune them in."

A little shiver went up her spine, a shiver that had nothing to do with being cold. What could he mean? Was he starting to care for her in a romantic way? In for a penny, she thought as she asked, "Why?"

His sensuous lips curled in a smile as he glanced at her, and said, "Aren't you direct? You're definitely not Asian."

He really was very good looking, thought Lorelei. Despite her recent travails, a familiar warm yearning feeling stirred in her loins. Remembering his gentle refusal at his apartment the night she had run from Tomas, she ignored it. Aloud she said, "Well, I'm about as far from being Asian as one can get."

Laughing a little, he said, "That you are." Pausing, he grew serious as he continued, "I see some things very clearly around you." Glancing often at her as he drove, he reminded her that she should look after herself. "Please, Lorelei, see a doctor; I see some trouble for you, some female trouble. I asked you about that before, remember?" She nodded as he repeated, "Please, humour me, and see a doctor. Promise?"

With so much sincere appeal in his voice, Lorelei could not refuse. "Yes, alright, I will. Are you always so concerned about the health of others?" Though Paula had affirmed that he was, she wanted to hear what Kwok Lee had to say.

He was silent, his eyes on the road. The sun had set, and in the twilight, she couldn't quite read his face. "No, not always. When I was a med student in England I was quite hedonistic and as selfish as they come. I was always a sensitive, in the spiritual sense, but I didn't pay it much attention. Studying allopathic medicine makes you suspicious of non-scientific ways of knowing things."

Kwok Lee, or Lee, as he was known then, had been a typical university student, spending his time studying and tasting of the sensual pleasures the world offers handsome young men of means.

"And then I met ... her. Lesley."

"Lesley?"

He sighed; a sound of longing and dreams unfulfilled. Lesley Mason had been a young art history student with whom he had fallen deeply in love. In her aura, he had seen the danger of a serious disease; she had laughed off his concerns until it was too late. Eventually, she had died in his arms. After that, he had abandoned studying western medicine in favour of traditional Asian healing.

"I needed to be where I could use my abilities and have them acknowledged."

So Paula had been right that he had suffered a great romantic hurt. Lorelei felt that he must be starting to trust her if he was letting her see him in this emotionally vulnerable state. "Kwok Lee?" she asked, tentatively. She would not ask her next question if he withdrew into himself.

"Yes?"

She couldn't see his face, but he sounded willing to continue the tenor of the conversation. Her voice soft, she asked, "Lesley. What was she like?" Lorelei half expected him to remain silent, but he surprised her.

Speaking quietly, almost to himself, he said, "She was rather like you. Petite, long red hair, sea green eyes.... And when she was determined to do something, nothing would get in her way. After she passed, she would come to me when I was meditating and tell me to get on with life."

Lorelei pulled the blanket tighter, thinking. She had never given much thought to the metaphysical, dismissing those who believed in such things as cranks. Until now, she had been the kind of person who had to see, hear, and touch something to believe in its reality. True, she had gone to church as a child, but had only considered each Sunday outing to be a social occasion, and when she was a teenager, she had fought to escape the church's enforced conformity. Kwok Lee was no crank, of that she was sure, and he seemed to have abilities that science could not explain. Perhaps she had missed something. She spent the remainder of the journey silently thinking. Kwok Lee seemed to understand, for he said nothing more.

It was fully dark when they arrived at Lorelei's home. Kwok Lee pulled the truck up to the curb in front of the house, and turned off the ignition. Lorelei made no move to get out of the vehicle. Turning to him, she said, "I'm not looking forward to explaining all this," indicating the blanket she was wrapped in and her sodden clothes on the floor.

"I'm coming in with you; your friends need to see that you have been cared for. I thank the fates that I chose today to visit my sister." His voice was low, full of emotion.

Her voice matched his as she whispered, "Thank you, Kwok Lee... I don't know what I would have done if you hadn't come along..." Tears threatened to escape her eyes; she swallowed hard as she fought for control. Even now, in the company of a man whom she knew would not be judgmental, she wanted to appear strong.

"Here, let's get you inside before you catch a chill. You should have a hot bath with some Epsom salts as soon as you can." Once they were out of the truck, she realized she couldn't walk across the sidewalk and up the gravelled walkway in her bare feet. Her soaking wet moccasins were useless. Kwok Lee quickly came to her side, and before she knew it, had swept her up in his arms.

"I'm sorry, I should have realized," he said.

He carried her easily, her head resting on his shoulder. It had been a very long time since she had felt so secure, if indeed she ever had. The scent of lemongrass clung to him, and something else, very male, that she could not identify. Despite being exhausted, she felt her body quiver in response to him. If he noticed, he did not acknowledge it as he approached the door, which opened before him.

As they entered the house, Lorelei blinked at the bright lights, and then her eyes focussed on first one familiar face, then another. Paula was at the door, closing it, while Myles came from the kitchen, having just hung up the phone.

As Kwok Lee set Lorelei on her feet, her friends started talking at once.

"Where have you been?" Myles began.

"When Cathi-Ann said she hadn't heard from you..." Paula said.

"We got worried..."

"Then your supervisor from work called..."

"Then we really got worried, especially since... well, we were worried," finished Myles, somewhat awkwardly.

"Time enough for the story later," said Kwok Lee, "right now, Lorelei needs a hot bath and probably something to eat."

Swaying a little, Lorelei almost fainted, before Paula quickly steadied her, and gently led her to the bathroom. Lorelei glanced over her shoulder at Kwok Lee, who smiled encouragement.

Paula started the bath for her, saying, "Have a nice long soak. When you're done, I'll make you something to eat while you tell us what happened."

The hot water was pure bliss after the day Lorelei had endured. When she emerged from the bathroom a half-hour later, wearing her old comfortable bathrobe, her hair in a towel, Kwok Lee had left. Paula was stirring something at the stove as she came into the kitchen and sat at the table.

"That smells delicious, what is it?" she asked.

"I made a beef stew for dinner tonight," Paula replied, as she filled a large soup plate and placed it before her.

Just then, Myles came downstairs from his room. "Well, you look better," he said, "any tea left in the pot, Paula?"

Though she felt rather nauseated, Lorelei forced herself to eat. Her roommates, cups of tea in front of them, waited patiently for her to finish. Feeling slightly better after she finished eating, Lorelei sipped her own tea. Looking at her friends, she realized that neither of them could quite make eye contact.

"What is it?" She remembered now that Myles had seemed about to say something when she had first come in with Kwok Lee. She saw Paula exchange glances with Myles before she said, "You tell her, Myles, you know Mei better than I."

"What? What about Mei?"

The young man set his cup down. His manner very serious, he told Lorelei that Tomas had gone to Mei's apartment the night before, then beat and raped her. Very few people knew, and Mei did not want anyone else to know, not even Michael Allison, with whom she had begun a relationship.

"Katy and her friend Samantha are helping her as much as they can... they tried to get her go to the police... but she wouldn't."

"Most rapes go unreported; the victims can't face the humiliation of being questioned," said Paula.

Lorelei was silent, her mind reeling. She could have prevented the attack, she was sure of it. She should have been thinking about other women Tomas was likely to be in contact with. Instead, once her own safety was restored, she had thought nothing more about the incident.

"Oh God," she said, propping her chin in her hands. "I should have said something, shouldn't I, Paula? You wanted me to, but I didn't listen."

"No one wants to believe anyone they know is dangerous, Lore," Paula said, gently.

"There's plenty of self-blaming going on. Katy and Samantha feel terrible; Sam waited for Mei, and when she didn't hear from her, she called Katy," explained Myles. He stood up. "I'm going to go over to Katy's. Oh, and maybe you should call C.A., she's called twice already."

After he had left, Paula said, "And maybe you should call your work, too."

Wearily, Lorelei asked, "Do you reckon I've lost the job?"

"I don't know, the only way to be certain is to bite the bullet and call."

Reluctantly, Lorelei called her supervisor, who was very annoyed with her. As it happened, she had not contravened any specific rule by going out with Carl on her own time, but it was pointed out that by doing so, her professional relationship with Carl had become blurred. Carl had returned to the house in some obvious emotional distress. It had taken some time, but the workers had finally gotten him to tell them what had happened, as he saw it. He had thought Lorelei had run away on a whim and come to harm. When he understood that Lorelei had been frightened by his delusional episode, he was quite contrite, and swore that he would never have hurt her. As it stood, the supervisor was certain that Lorelei would find it difficult to recapture the worker-client relationship. Lorelei was expecting to be fired; she was surprised when she was told that, since it would take some time to find Carl another group home, Lorelei could have the following week off.

Hanging up the phone, she almost wept in relief. The income from the job wasn't a lot, but without it, she would be in dire straits until David decided to be reasonable about the divorce settlement. Returning to the chair where she had been sitting, she suddenly felt extremely fatigued. Her back ached, and she stumbled.

Quickly, Paula caught her, and half carried her to her bed. "You'd better get some rest, Lore, before you do yourself more harm."

Lorelei crawled into the warm cocoon of her bed. "Oh, no," she said.

"I forgot about Cathi-Ann."

"I'll call her."

"Oh would you?" Lorelei felt herself drifting as she murmured, "Thank you." She did not hear Paula's reply as she happily gave herself to the welcome oblivion of sleep.

– Chapter Six –

Over the course of the next few days, Lorelei learned that Tomas seemed to have disappeared, and that Mei had shut herself away in her apartment, and was only willing to see her very closest friends. Lorelei tried to focus on what Paula had said, that most people did not want to recognize that someone they knew could pose a danger to others, but she could not stop herself from feeling somehow responsible for what had happened. She felt discombobulated, and devoid of confidence; feelings she was not used to having, or at least, not acknowledging, even to herself.

The days were lengthening as late April moved into May. Lorelei was due to return to work at the group home, but she did not feel ready. Reluctantly, she asked for another week off; the need for time to sort herself out outweighed the need for money, at least for now.

Lorelei tried to immerse herself in her artwork, going on one occasion to the large municipal art gallery where there was a major exhibition of serigraphs. Under other circumstances, she would have found the large, bold silkscreen prints very inspiring, but this time, they were no more thought provoking to her than a blank wall.

While her roommates came and went with the busy-ness of their lives, Lorelei felt caught in a slow-moving time warp. She took to lying on her bed staring at the ceiling, thinking of nothing, which is what she was doing when one day, Cathi-Ann knocked on the door. Letting herself in, the dark-haired young woman called, "Lore? Are you okay?"

"In here," Lorelei replied.

Cathi-Ann stood in the doorway to Lorelei's room, her hands on her hips. "Lore, this isn't like you. What's up?"

At that moment, Lorelei was glad that Cathi-Ann wasn't the most intuitive person in the world; she did not want to give voice to the guilt that she felt about Mei, nor to the fear concerning the promise she had made to Kwok Lee. She had indeed gone to her doctor and had undergone some tests, all without her friends' knowledge, and this afternoon, she had received the diagnosis.

Aloud, she said, "Oh, I don't know. Just fretting, I reckon."

"Well, hey, why don't you come with me to Jingle Shell Beach? Some people I know are camping there. It'll be fun."

Ordinarily, Lorelei leapt at any chance to get out, be among people, and have fun. If she refused, Cathi-Ann would know there was something wrong, and if she went, she worried that she would not be able to appear to be her usual self amongst a group of people. Deciding that perhaps the distraction would be good for her, she said, "Alright, let's go then." Getting off the bed, she glanced in the mirror; her old green Indian print dress was fine for the beach. She slipped on a pair of sandals and they were on their way.

During the drive, Lorelei was quiet, thankful that Cathi-Ann, in her chatty way, filled the time, seemingly unaware of Lorelei's silence. She wasn't paying much attention until Cathi-Ann said, "Oh yeah, and you know that Mei girl?"

With a sense of dread, Lorelei said, slowly, "Ye-es."

"For some reason she tried to kill herself the other night…didn't Myles tell you?"

Lorelei shook her head. Maybe that was why she hadn't seen him for a few days.

"She took pills…but she was found in time. She's in the hospital now."

The world swirled around her; Lorelei felt like she couldn't breathe; she quietly fought for control while she was screaming inside. Mei had tried to kill herself! And *she* could have prevented it! This, on top of everything else! She swallowed hard, and forced herself to breathe slowly. Cathi-Ann did not notice, as she was concentrating on driving down the long winding road from the highway to the beach while speculating on why Mei could have done what she did.

"It'll be a man, for sure, it always is."

Cathi-Ann was right, but not in the way that she assumed. Lorelei made no reply as her friend parked the car. Once they were walking toward the camping area, Lorelei realized she still had no desire to socialize. She told her friend that she was going to go for a walk, and headed towards the water as Cathi-Ann made off towards her friends, who were building a campfire some way down the beach.

The tide was receding, leaving a vast expanse of glittering sand in its wake. Lorelei walked toward the distant water, sandals in hand, paying no heed to the many types of seashells that littered the beach, or to the large flocks of herring gulls that soared overhead. She had too much to think about. Though she had been told the prognosis for her condition was quite good, she felt as if the past few days comprised the last scenes of a dark and sad movie. What good had she ever done to anyone? David had tried, in his distant way, to make her happy, and she had not acknowledged it. Instead, she had lashed out in anger, destroying any chance they ever had of understanding each other.

And then there was Tomas. Her friends did not blame her for what he had done to Mei, but Lorelei still felt as if she could have done something, could have warned Mei somehow, for she knew that Tomas had wanted Mei. And now the poor girl was in hospital, having tried to commit suicide, and she, Lorelei was responsible for that near-tragedy. If only she had said something… and now she had ovarian cancer. It was in the very early stages, but Dr. Francis had told her that it required a series of debilitating treatments which would make her feel horrible. What was the point? It was cancer, which would probably kill her in the end. No more divorce struggle for David, no more cruel lovers for her.

Studying art had been exciting at first; then she had become aware of how phenomenally talented some of her classmates were and had suffered extreme self doubt, though no one knew it. Despite selling some prints at the student show, she felt overshadowed by the large impressive works of students like Mei Lundgren. How could she compete? Really, the only positive thing that had occurred in her life for a long while was meeting Kwok Lee, who carried his own pain, but had somehow channelled it into doing good works for other people. And he had refused her; gently, to be sure, but it was a refusal all the same.

Lorelei reached the water. Hiking her long green skirt up, she began to wade through the surprisingly warm wavelets that lapped the olive-green sands. She looked toward the distant high tide area where Cathi-Ann and her friends were enjoying a marshmallow roast, feeling no connection to the festivities. Wading on, she held her skirt higher as the water now came to her knees.

Suddenly, Lorelei's feet slipped out from under her. For a moment, arms wildly flailing, she tried to regain her footing, but it was useless;

she fell beneath the deep green waters. She'd stepped over a drop-off! At first she did not panic, as she was a strong swimmer, but a few seconds later, she realized that the undertow was pulling her down. Lorelei held her breath as she struggled desperately toward the mirrored surface she could see not three feet above her, but became entangled in a forest of seaweed, her red hair streaming out behind her. Unable to hold her breath any longer, she exhaled, sending a silver stream of bubbles carrying the last of her life-essence away. Then she was aware of a choking, coughing sensation before the universe went black.

This was strange. Lorelei could see herself, floating within the ribbons of seaweed like a sea nymph, her green dress undulating with the current, her eyes wide open, her lips pursed in surprise. Her view changed from one parallel with the body in the water, to an aerial perspective. A boat with two men aboard had appeared; one of the men leaped into the water. She watched as they pulled the body aboard and sped away. For a moment, she wondered if she should follow them.

Her view changed again as she beheld her parents, sitting in the kitchen of their house on the family sheep station in Australia. They were just beginning to eat breakfast. Lorelei felt deep sorrow for them, beginning another ordinary day without knowing what had happened to their daughter. They had loved her in the only way they could, she was now sure.

Suddenly, Lorelei was standing on a grassy verge overlooking a beautiful sunlit valley. She watched as huge, iridescent birds soared through an impossibly blue sky. Music that sounded like a crystalline xylophone seemed to emanate from the very air. Where was she? From behind, she heard a dog joyfully barking. Lorelei turned to see…no, it couldn't be! It was Roo, her beloved blue heeler dog from her childhood, but Roo had died of old age when she was fourteen years old.

"Roo!" she cried, realizing that she did not need to speak aloud to be heard. She *was* dead, and this was heaven if Roo was here. "Did you love me as much as I loved you?"

In her head, she heard the joyous reply, "Yes!" before the dog scampered off, chasing ethereal butterflies. That was her Roo, alright; he had always loved chasing flying things. She watched indulgently as he danced through the grass. Gradually she became aware of a presence to her left. Looking toward it, she saw Kwok Lee standing there, clad in luminescent blue silk, dark hair flowing in golden heaven-light, like an Asian Messiah. How could this be?

"Lorelei," he said, his lips unmoving. The deep voice seemed to come from all around her. "It's not your time."

"Kwok Lee, how can you…"

"You must go back, it's not your time," he repeated.

Small glittering orbs began to appear all around her like soap bubbles. Each one held a scene from her life; there was the time when she was ten, when she had taunted another girl for being overweight; at fifteen, when in an adolescent fury, she had told her mother that she was the worse mother in the world; and more recently, there was David, when she had screamed at him that he was a boring excuse for a husband. She felt all their pain, yet it was not unbearable. It was somehow comforting, knowing that she could still feel.

A new, larger orb approached her, growing bigger as it came. In it, she could see two doctors and a nurse feverishly working above a still, white form. What a strange looking thing it was, lying on the gurney. She looked towards Kwok Lee, who nodded. A deep sense of inner peace seemed to envelop her. His voice sounded again.

"Go back. I will be there. Go back."

The orb was as big as a doorway now. She stepped, or floated, into it, finding herself above the tableau that was playing out before her. As if someone was turning up the volume on a television set, she became aware of the noise of the room.

"Even if she survives, she'll be a vegetable, she's gone without oxygen for far too long," said the shorter of the two doctors.

"Damn!" said the other doctor. "Dr. Saunders, you're right. Pronounce death at three thirty three p.m. Damn!"

"Why are you so upset?" said the first doctor. Looking at the pale body still clad in the sodden green dress. "She's just another hippie. No loss to mankind." He turned to go. The other doctor had already left.

That did it. Lorelei's spirit-self leaped back into the still body and willed it to live. Slipping into a black nothingness, she had no awareness of how much time had passed when she began to be aware of a feeling of pressure on her chest. Only half-conscious, she coughed up a large amount of water as a nurse leaped to her side.

"Dr. Saunders! She's alive!" cried the nurse, as she steadied Lorelei, who was almost throwing herself to the floor with violent coughing spasms. After a minute or two the coughing began to subside.

The doctor took her pulse, saying, "Well, young lady, you've defied science and had a lucky escape. You were clinically dead." His manner was stiffly professional, and gave no hint of the miracle that had just taken place.

Her voice raspy, she said, "I...I heard what you said...you ... you said that I was no loss. You bastard!" She spat the last word.

The doctor blanched, but did not acknowledge what she had said.

His back to her, he gave the nurse some instructions, and then he was gone. She was too weak to complain as she was moved, somewhat perfunctorily, to a semi-private room where she immediately fell into a deep sleep.

— Chapter Seven —

Lorelei came to with a start. Confused, she looked around her, not knowing where she was, before she began to remember what had happened. Conflicting emotions assailed her. Had it been real? If it was, she wanted to go back to the deep love and warmth of that mystical place of total acceptance and peace. How unfair that she should have but a little taste of it, then have it snatched away, especially now, when she had seen how she had unintentionally hurt others. And yet, she was also very angry. That idiot doctor! How dare he just write her off as if she was no more than a piece of driftwood!

The room was very quiet, the other bed being unoccupied. There was nothing on the bedside table to indicate that anyone other than medical personnel had been to see her, so she could not have been asleep for very long. As nurses and orderlies began to make their rounds, she was astounded to find that it was the morning after the day she had drowned. When Dr. Francis came to examine her, she did not mention her experience, nor did he, except to say that sometimes, for inexplicable reasons, people survived situations which should have killed them. He also reminded her that she would need to start treatment for the ovarian cancer very soon.

Lorelei had fallen asleep again when a slight noise made her open her eyes; there was Kwok Lee standing in the doorway. With the bright lights of the hallway behind him, he seemed to be standing in an aura of golden light. She blinked, unsure that he was actually there. He came closer. Gently pushing her hair out of her eyes, he said, "How are you?"

Such simple words; millions spoke them every day as a standard greeting, with no expectation that the words would be taken literally. The way Kwok Lee pronounced them, with deep layers of empathy in his voice and eyes, made Lorelei tremble. As he bent towards her, she caught the licorice-sweet scent of fivespice.

"I suppose I'm alright. I…I…it must have been a dream. They said I was dead…the…the damn doctor said I was no loss…and it doesn't look like anyone but you have been to see me."

The tears that she had been holding back for so long began to flow down her pale cheeks. Kwok Lee took her hand in his, and just stood by silently while she cried. After some minutes, her sobs abated.

"Was it really a dream when I saw …when I saw those men pull me out of the water…but how could it be a dream…they said I was dead…am I crazy?"

Still holding her hand, Kwok Lee smiled, and said, "No, you're not crazy. You've just had a very profound spiritual experience." He went on to explain that it was called a near death experience, and people often saw dead friends and relatives while having one. Many such events went unreported, out of fear of ridicule. "Modern science does not yet accept the reality of the soul," he said.

Lorelei did not know what to make of this, grounded as she was in the material world, yet she knew what she had seen. "I saw the dog I had when I was a kid. I asked him if he loved me as much as I loved him. He said yes. How is that possible?"

"Dogs are intelligent beings, if the capacity for love is the qualification for intelligence. Love is what connects us, here and in the after life."

Lorelei wanted to believe this, but the cynic in her was doubtful. Until now, love had been synonymous with sex, but maybe there was something deeper in it, maybe there were different kinds of love. And there was something else, just on the edge of her memory. Like a light going on, she suddenly remembered. "Ohhhh, I saw you! But you're not dead! How could I have seen you?"

Kwok Lee explained that he had been meditating, and in that state, it was possible to see people who had passed away, though he had only been thinking of her, and trying to send some positive energy her way to help her gather the strength to face her illness.

She fiddled with the bedcovers, not looking at him. Quietly, she said, "Then you know. You know its cancer. And you knew before… before I was diagnosed."

"Not specifically that it was cancer, but that it was serious, and which system was involved. Have they talked to you about treatment yet?"

Lorelei did not answer. She was terrified of the prospect of chemotherapy, which meant that she would have to endure being very ill after each treatment, after which she would be able to do nothing more than rest and gather her strength for the next session.

Her face betrayed her fear, for Kwok Lee said, ""I see that they have. There are alternatives, Lorelei. We'll talk of those later."

As she looked into his calm slate-blue eyes, eyes that radiated quiet concern, spark of hope flickered inside Lorelei. He seemed so certain; maybe there really was a less drastic form of treatment for her illness. Paula seemed to believe in him, and so far, he was the only person who had bothered to come to the hospital to see her. Maybe she should explore the possibilities of eastern medicine. She pushed away the thought, not wanting to make a decision at that moment.

Aloud, she said somewhat petulantly, "And you're the only person who has come to see me. I don't understand why Cathi-Ann hasn't been here." She looked at Kwok Lee, unaware of how vulnerable she looked, like a small child lying in bed, home from school with a bad cold. He seemed to be far away, lost in thought, absently twirling a lock of her hair around his finger. She forgot herself as she realized he must be thinking of Lesley, the girl he had loved, who had died. Lorelei did not like to see him look so sad, but could not bring herself to ask him about it. Instead, she simply said, "Kwok Lee?"

Startled, he said, "Oh, sorry. You were saying...?"

"Cathi-Ann hasn't come to see me."

"Paula has spoken to her. It seems she feels a bit guilty for persuading you to go with her."

That made her feel somewhat better, but something still bothered her. "Like I do about Mei...she's here, too...in the hospital. Kwok Lee, I need to apologize to her; if I had told her what Tomas had done to me..."

"I suspect she's enough to contend with right now, and you don't know what the man would have done even if you had not seen him that night. His karma will catch up to him."

She sighed. "I expect you're right. I just...I wonder where everyone is....Paula...I need to see Paula, I think I've lost my job..."

"I'm sure she'll be along..." he broke off, as someone came into the room.

"Talk of the devil," said Lorelei, as Paula approached her. "I was just saying that I need to see you."

The tall young woman looked apologetic. "I'm sorry, Lore; I've been pulling twelve-hour shifts at the Crisis Line. I didn't know anything until Kwok Lee here called me this morning, and then I called Cathi-Ann." She set a potted African violet on the bedside table. "Here's a little something to cheer you up," she said.

"Thank you, Paula. Besides the two of you, no one else has been here." She still couldn't believe that more people hadn't been in to see her. Here she had been dead, actually dead; her room should be filled with flowers and gifts, and instead, only Paula and Kwok Lee had come.

"Well, Myles feels bad enough about Mei, and with you here, too… he's just immersed himself in his work. Cathi-Ann feels guilty, I know, but I'm sure she'll be along soon. When I heard what happened, I couldn't believe it."

"I still can't," said Lorelei, unsure as to whether or not she should tell her friend about her near death experience.

Kwok Lee stood up, smiling. "I sense some girl talk approaching, and I do have clients to see. Lorelei, when you're discharged, let me know, and if you need a ride home, just call."

"Alright…and thank you, Kwok Lee." Something in the way she spoke to him made Paula look at her, curious. Once the young man had left, she said, "What was that about, the thank you?"

"That's a bit of a story," Lorelei replied, fidgeting.

"I'd like to hear it. You look a little restless. I noticed a sitting room nearby. Do you want to go there?" Paula helped her out of the bed and led her to the sunny, cheerful room. It was furnished with home-like couches and armchairs and painted in tasteful, warm colours. Once they were comfortable, Lorelei described what had happened, including the near death experience.

"And I…felt how other people had felt about things I have done…"

"Don't let it get to you, Lorelei. I've heard of this; if it's meant to do anything, it's meant to help you take stock of life, maybe make some decisions."

"You reckon?"

"Yes. And you saw Kwok Lee?"

"I did, yeah. He said he was meditating, trying to send me good energy, whatever that means."

"It means he cares enough to take the time to do it. And look what he's already done for you."

"I dunno. He's been very nice to me so far, but…he's still a man, and after David, and the other losers I've hooked up with…"

"Well, if I know one thing, it is this; Kwok Lee is truly a healer, he has helped people who got help nowhere else. And he's not likely to make a move on you."

Paula's words seemed to reverberate in Lorelei's head. She considered telling her roommate about her illness, but thought better of it. Kwok Lee had said that there were alternatives; she needed to know what those were before she would let anyone know what she was going through. From Paula she learned that her employer was holding her job open for her, and that David had seemed unconcerned when Paula had called him with news of Lorelei's accident.

Whatever sympathy she had felt for David after her near death experience vanished with this news. "I can imagine his disappointment when I didn't die," she said, rather bitterly. "It's still going to cost him money to get the divorce settled." She looked at Paula. "You know what? I'm going to tell him he can have everything. It's not worth fighting anymore. I have the only thing I really wanted, which is out."

"That would settle one issue for you, wouldn't it?"

"Yes, it would. I think it would frustrate him more, really." She slumped in her seat, as a sudden fatigue overcame her.

"Here, I think it's time to go back to bed, Lore," Paula said, putting her arm around her. Lorelei let Paula guide her back to her room. Looking down the long hallway, she saw a lithe young man with flowing dark hair enter a room just past the nurses' station.

"I knew it! That's Michael Allison, the singer, going to see Mei. I knew she had something going with him."

As Paula helped her onto the bed, she laughed a little as she said, "You must be feeling a bit better if you're interested in sexual intrigue again."

"I'll have to be dead for good before I'm not interested in such things," Lorelei laughed back, albeit somewhat weakly.

Once Lorelei was settled in the bed, Paula regarded her affectionately for a few seconds before saying, "I'd better leave you to rest. Call the house if you need anything, okay?"

After she had gone, Lorelei lay thinking. So much had happened in past few days; she was now aware of things she had never before acknowledged. It was a revelation to realize that she was capable of hurting another person. Of course, she had been intellectually aware of the possibility, but to really feel another's emotional pain, pain that she had caused, was another story. Yes, she would tell David he could have everything. Lorelei wasn't particularly materialistic, so it did not feel like a capitulation. She had been fighting David mostly to be a thorn in his side, taking pleasure in annoying him. Paula was right; it would settle the problem and perhaps give her a feeling of completion.

How different Paula was from herself. Lorelei had never really understood Paula's desire to help others, but after being on the receiving end of her concern, Lorelei was beginning to gain some insight into her friend. Remembering how she had derided Paula's choice of profession, she felt a twinge of guilt. Paula always put everyone else before herself; and had been a good friend to her, better than many.

Cathi-Ann was one of them. Now that she thought about it, her outspoken friend was good company at a party, but not inclined to be emotionally supportive when the chips were down. She was more likely to encourage a depressed person to go out and have a good time, which Lorelei now understood she was doing the day they had gone to the beach. Cathi-Ann just didn't understand what was involved in depression, and didn't seem to care, either. So unlike Kwok Lee or Paula.

What had Kwok Lee said? That there were other possibilities for treatment of her cancer? Could it be true? And if she decided to let him help her, would it work? What if it didn't and she died? She might die anyway, and what would that do to Kwok Lee after loving and losing Lesley? He would be saddened, but he would accept it in his Confucian way. And if he was right, communication was possible with those who had died. She wondered if Lesley still made her presence known to him.

She could die. She could really die. A shuddering sigh escaped her. She wanted to cry again, but somehow the tears would not come. How awful to die without ever having felt loved. Yes, she knew her parents loved her, and David had professed to love her, but she had never *felt* loved. Was it her fault? Was the reason she was suspicious of empathetic people like Kwok Lee and Paula because she believed herself to be unlovable?

She shook herself. No! She was Lorelei McMillan, flame-haired siren, destroyer of men. That was a far more comforting thought. If Kwok Lee had information that could be of any value, she would use it. He was emotionally wounded, and she was glad he was celibate. That way, she could use him for his expertise without sex getting in the way, though she still found him very attractive. Well, even I can't have everyone, she thought.

Confined to bed as she was, Lorelei was starting to feel restless. The bustling, efficient nurses and other hospital staff made her want to scream. Lorelei was relieved to hear that she would be discharged the following morning, with the promise that she would begin chemotherapy very soon. She wasn't sure whom she would call to give her a ride home; she would decide that on the morrow.

— Chapter Eight —

Lorelei stirred, unwilling to wake up, having been in the midst of a beautiful dream, one in which she was enveloped in a cocoon of love in a universe of light. Reluctantly, she turned over and opened her eyes. She sighed; at least she was in her own room, and the house was quiet, which was a relief after the noisy routine of the hospital.

No one had been home when she had arrived early yesterday afternoon. With characteristic independence, she had decided against calling anyone to take her home from the hospital. Instead, she had taken a taxi, despite the expense. Lorelei had gone out for a few hours, and when she had returned, the house was still empty. She had turned in for the evening without calling anyone, and having fallen into a deep sleep, did not hear anyone come home. For all she knew, she was still alone in the house.

She didn't want to get out of bed, for once she did, the lingering dream-world warmth would dissipate, and she would have to face her reality. Yesterday she had managed to take care of a couple of important things; she had visited her employer and after extracting a promise of confidentiality, had explained the state of her health. The supervisor in turn had offered to put her on the on-call list, for unlike regularly scheduled workers, she would then have the option of turning down a shift if her health demanded that she rest. Lorelei had been very relieved, as she had expected to lose the job, and the income that went with it. If she was able to work, even a little, she would not feel as helpless as she otherwise would.

She had also seen her lawyer, who had been surprised at her request to let David know she was no longer interested in arguing over material things. It all seemed so pointless now, though Lorelei did have some second thoughts. Though she had elected not to drive, by rights, she was entitled to one of the cars, which she could sell. No, she would show David that getting shut of him was what she really wanted. Lorelei was discovering that Paula had been right; she was beginning to feel that the David chapter of her life was coming to an end. Chuckling faintly, she imagined the look of surprise on David's face when he received the news; she only wished she could see it in person.

The noise of movement in the kitchen told her that at least one of her roommates was in the house. Soon Lorelei could hear the kettle whistling; signalling not only boiling water, but also that Paula was the one who was up, as she often preferred tea to coffee in the mornings. Getting out of bed, Lorelei wrapped her old robe around herself and went into the kitchen where Paula, startled at seeing her, nearly spilled her tea.

"Lorelei!" she exclaimed. "When did you get home? And why didn't you call?"

Taking a seat at the kitchen table, she replied, "I didn't want to bother anyone; I came home yesterday afternoon."

"Want some tea?" asked Paula.

Lorelei nodded. "Thanks," she said, as a cup was passed to her.

"Have you been sleeping the whole time?"

"No," she replied. She explained what she had done the day before.

"You don't let the grass grow under your feet do you? You didn't overextend yourself? You look a little tired."

Lorelei considered telling Paula about having cancer, but she could not bear to receive the sympathy she knew Paula would lavish upon her. She replied, "Just getting settled in again. The hospital is so noisy it's hard to stay asleep."

"What are you going to do today?" asked Paula, as she put bread in the toaster.

"I don't know. I reckon I should call Kwok Lee."

"Yes, he seems to like you, Lorelei."

"I know. I'm a bit worried about that," she admitted. At the question in the tall girl's face, she explained about Lesley. "You were right, Paula, he's suffered in the past and this is his way of dealing with it."

"Maybe he's just not past the grieving yet. For sensitive people, it can take a long time before they are ready for another relationship."

"So you think there's hope?"

The toaster popped; Paula applied butter and jam and handed one slice to Lorelei. "Don't even think about it! Let the poor guy be, surely there are others you can prey on!"

"No, no, I meant for him, not me," Lorelei protested as she began to eat.

Paula blinked. "Is this the same Lorelei McMillan who once said that the male species was like a smorgasbord and that satiating yourself on the most delicious dishes was your mission in life?" she said, laughing. Her manner more serious, she said softly, "Your experience has really affected you, hasn't it?"

Again Lorelei thought of telling Paula about her cancer, and again she decided against it. Better to have her think her drowning experience was entirely to blame for any changes in her manner or outlook. "Yeah, I reckon it has," she said, sighing sadly.

"What's wrong?"

"Oh, Cathi-Ann. She didn't come to the hospital…has she called here?" At least she could use her disappointment in Cathi-Ann as a plausible excuse for her sadness.

"No, she hasn't. I'm sure you'll hear from her."

"Hmmm, I don't know if I want to now."

"Well, you'll sort it out. You've been friends a long time," Paula, ever the optimist, replied. She gulped the last of her tea, and then put the cup in the sink. "I must go. Myles is at Katy's and I don't know when he'll be back." She grabbed her purse from the counter, and headed for the front door. "Bye for now!"

Lorelei heard her say hello to someone as she went out; a moment later, Kwok Lee appeared in the kitchen, carrying a package. He was clad in jeans, sandals, and a white tank shirt instead of the usual Chinese silk robe. His honey-coloured skin was tanned a deep bronze, and the snug-fitting shirt revealed his tightly-muscled chest. Dressed this way, and with his long wavy hair brushing his shoulders, he reminded her of Michael Allison, the rock singer, except he was more exotic, and to her, far more attractive. He set the package on the table. Leaning against the counter, he said, "I called the hospital to find that you'd gone home. Did Paula come get you?"

"No, no, I just decided to come home by taxi," she said, expecting him to protest that he would have given her a ride home. She was surprised when he merely stood listening to her, a neutral expression on his face. It was times like this, when Kwok Lee did not behave as most other men she had known would, that she found him most fascinating. If he really cared, shouldn't he be shouting at her, berating her for taking a chance with her health in coming home from the hospital on her own? Instead, he simply accepted her explanation without comment.

She turned her large, beryl-green eyes to him and read the question in his eyes. Knowing what it was, and not yet ready to answer it, she indicated the package on the table and asked, "What is this?"

He smiled slightly. She had the distinct impression that he was humouring her. "The clothing you were wearing the day you had your adventure in the woods. They've been washed, although I'm afraid your suede jacket was not salvageable," he said.

Lorelei opened the brown paper-wrapped package to reveal what she wore the day she had gone out with Carl. Not being one who was easily embarrassed, she was surprised to feel her cheeks flush as she found her black lace underthings tucked between the neatly folded jeans and shirt.

Nonplussed, she stammered, "Oh…oh…thank you…you didn't have to…"

"It was the least I could do, Lorelei…" he said, softly.

She fought for control as tears welled in her eyes; she so hated anyone to see that she was vulnerable, but Kwok Lee was different. "You…did so much for me that day…and now…I know why you're here…you want to talk about the cancer…" and then she started crying, softly at first, then deep, heaving sobs that gave voice to the terror she had been trying to keep hidden.

Instantly, Kwok Lee was at her side, and before Lorelei could protest, had swept her up in his arms and had moved to the living room, where he sat with her on his lap. He rocked her back and forth like a child while she cried. Many minutes later, her sobs began to subside; a few minutes more, and she was cried out. Still, he had not spoken. She heaved one last sob-breath and snuggled against him. This was the second time she had been this close to him; she felt safe, and somehow not as afraid of what the future held. Sighing again, she became conscious of the scent of jasmine that clung to his hair. She slid off his lap onto the other side of the couch.

"Oh!" she exclaimed.

"I'm sorry…have I embarrassed you?"

"No…I just…I haven't even brushed my teeth. I'm a mess!"

"Well, you're a nice mess," he said. "Why don't you get ready, and I'll take you back to mine and I'll make you breakfast."

"I'd like that," she said. "It won't take me long to clean up and get dressed."

Lorelei showered quickly, then looked in her closet, and tried to decide what to wear. Ordinarily, if she was going to be in the company of a handsome man, she would dress in a very provocative manner, but she knew that Kwok Lee would only ignore her sexual signals. Still, she wanted to look attractive. After rejecting several choices, she finally settled on a cobalt blue long-sleeved knit top and a pair of high-waisted pocketless jeans that were figure hugging without being too tight.

She brushed out her hair, and then struggled to clip the thick terra-cotta tresses back with a large green, dragonfly-shaped abalone barrette. Then she applied minimal amounts of eyeliner, mascara, and lip-gloss to her face. Lorelei was always careful about the amount of makeup she wore, for she did not want to resemble a classmate who wore so much mascara that Lorelei thought she looked ridiculous.

As Kwok Lee was so tall that she was self-conscious about her small size, she slipped on a pair of high-heeled ankle boots and inspected her reflection in the bedroom mirror. She smiled at herself; with her hair pulled back, and the high-necked top, she looked demurely sexy, if such a thing was possible. Her smile vanished as a slight twinge in her abdomen that was not quite pain reminded her of the cancer's presence in her body. It was like having a strange alien being inside her, and before the day was out, she would have to make a decision about what to do about it.

Though Kwok Lee had just seen her in a vulnerable state, and she knew she had nothing to fear from him, Lorelei was slightly embarrassed at her earlier emotional display. She took a deep breath, squared her shoulders, and stepped brightly out into the living room. As she did so, she saw that Kwok Lee was standing with his back to her, looking out the living room window. He turned; on beholding her, his eyes widened. Lorelei expected, as had happened often with other men, an effusive comment on her beauty. However, he merely smiled and said, "Ready?"

He really didn't need to say anything. Lorelei was beginning to understand that he was attracted to her on a different level from that of all other men she had known, which only added to his mystique. Once they had arrived at his apartment, she learned that he employed a student a few mornings a week in the shop. She sat at the small teakwood table in the kitchen while he prepared food for her. "Having someone in the store gives me time to catch up on things...and allows me to work with a few people that need close guidance in their treatment."

Lorelei felt a pang of jealousy at this statement. Was she simply one more client with a particularly challenging disease? Aloud, she said, "Like me?"

He glanced at her as he worked. "No, not a bit like you," he said, rather softly.

Satisfied with his answer, and smiling rather smugly to herself, she remained silent until he began to place dishes in front of her. She looked at the large plate of sliced fruit, recognizing some as tropical fruits common in Australia.

"Oh, litchees! I haven't seen these in a while!"

" 'Lye-chees?' I've never heard it said that way," he teased. "My family always pronounced it 'lee-chees.'"

"Well I'm a strange foreigner," she said, reaching for a slice of melon.

"So am I," he replied. They both laughed at that.

"What's this custardy stuff in the dish? And these cracker things?"

"Brown rice wafers; much better for you than processed, yeasty wheat bread. And the stuff in the dish is durian fruit."

"Oh, I have heard of those. I think they grow them in northern Australia. They're really smelly when you open them up, aren't they?"

"Yes, they are. You don't want to open one on a hot day in the house. The smell lingers. The part you eat sweet and very flavourful," he said, as he placed a large, steaming mug front of her.

"Oh, the cleansing tea," she said, remembering what he had served her the other time she had been in his apartment. "What are you drinking? And why can't I have some of that?" she said, indicating the mug of steaming, dark brown-red liquid he held.

"Peu-erh tea, red tea. Very strong, and too acidic for you. You are going to have to avoid acidic foods altogether as part of your therapy." He hesitated, giving her an opportunity to decide whether or not she was ready to talk about treating her cancer.

Lorelei ate in silence for a moment, delaying the inevitable. They had been bantering like two people who knew each other well, and she had been enjoying it so much that she had actually forgotten for a few minutes that she had a serious condition. There was no getting away from it; she would have to face it sooner or later. She sighed, saying, "What else would I have to do?"

He leaned toward her, obviously eager to start. "A number of things," he replied. "I know it can be difficult, but I'll be here to help. You must abstain from all dairy products and meats, which contain toxins that will only add to your problems, and no coffee or alcohol."

"Wh...what?" she stuttered, nearly choking on a mouthful of fruit. She drank a few sips of her tea before she spoke again. "But I love a good steak or leg of lamb! And ice cream, and cheese. What about fish?"

"No meat at all," he said, with an air of authority.

Lorelei stopped eating, and slumped in her seat. A complete change of diet was unexpected; vitamins and such, yes, but not this. She had never been one who had to watch what she ate in terms of weight; she ate what she liked and never gave it a second thought. She stared at the plate in front of her, not wanting to meet Kwok Lee's eyes. In a small voice, she said, "I don't know if I can do all that." Fearfully, she turned sad green eyes to him.

He regarded her kindly and said, "I know it's hard to take in, but I will be here to help. The alternative is chemotherapy, which you know would be far more difficult. And I should tell you now; you will feel worse before you feel better. When you eliminate all toxin-producing elements from your diet, the toxins that are already in your body take some time to disappear from your system. This process will manifest itself as feeling very unwell, but nothing like what you would experience with chemotherapy."

Treatment for her cancer would also involve massage every a day that would 'align her energies' and slow down cell damage. The disease meant that her body was very acidic, thus she would have to stick to the diet and take digestive supplements to correct the acid balance in her body. Meditation would also be beneficial; he would help her in learning to do this.

"And one more thing," he said slowly. "You must abstain from sex." He looked at her meaningfully.

Lorelei shivered as he spoke. It was as if he could see into her very being. How could he know about her rather promiscuous behaviour of the past year or so? Or maybe he had just heard some gossip, which was the least of her worries. A cold sensation in the pit of her stomach spread to her extremities as she realized how much would have to change if she followed Kwok Lee's recommendations, and if she didn't follow through, she would have to endure the agony of chemotherapy.

"Oh!" Lorelei exclaimed as something else occurred to her.

Kwok Lee looked at her, curious. "What is it?"

"All of this…that you said I should do; all of this costs a lot of money, doesn't it? And I don't have any…Kwok Lee…I can't do it…"

"Chemo can cost money, too," he said. He looked thoughtful. "How are you at paperwork; bookkeeping, appointments, ordering, that sort of thing?"

Lorelei blinked in surprise at his question. "I've done that kind of work before; I used to work in a doctor's office."

"Well, why don't you come and do that for me? I'm hopeless … it all piles up and then I end up staying up late in order to sort it all out." He looked at her, his gaze unwavering.

Lorelei considered the offer. If she took him up on it, she could tell people that she was working at the shop, which would dispel any curiosity about why she was spending so much time there. She did not know which she feared most; the possibility of becoming a social pariah because of the dreaded disease, or being on the receiving end of unwanted sympathy.

"Alright," she said, "but I keep the job at the group home."

He laughed, a musical, yet still masculine sound that sent a delicious shiver through her body, despite her worries about her health. "It's a deal, but if I feel you are taking too much on, I will be the first to say so."

"When do I start?"

"How about tomorrow? I'll give you some of the supplements you need to start, and when you're here tomorrow, we'll go over the diet together, okay?" He paused. "How do you feel?"

Lorelei took a deep breath. "Relieved, I think, now that I know what I'm going to do. Um, I think I'd like to go home now, if that's alright with you, Kwok Lee."

She helped him clean up, and then followed him downstairs to the shop, where he gathered together the dietary supplements he had recommended. She listened attentively to him while he explained how often to take each of them, and what their function was. This part of the treatment was straightforward; she would have no problem remembering to take tablets and capsules, but the rest of it still intimidated her. Lorelei said as much, whereupon Kwok Lee gave her a vegetarian cookbook for her to study; and even pointed out recipes that he thought would be of particular benefit. He would have driven her home, but Lorelei preferred to make her own way there; it would give her some time to reflect on Kwok Lee's instructions, and, for that matter, Kwok Lee himself.

Chapter Nine

It was early afternoon when Lorelei reached home, where she met Myles, who was just leaving, on the wide front porch.

"Oh hi, are you okay now?" the young man asked, concern plain on his face.

What a loaded question, Lorelei thought, saying, "Oh yes, no lasting damage." Wanting to deflect his attention, she continued, "How is Mei doing?"

He brightened. "She's getting better, with Katy's help. I hear Michael Allison is looking after her. Hey, did I tell you I got some great photos of his ex-wife and Mei having an altercation at Dave's Marina at Sapphire Bay?"

"No, I've hardly seen you this last little while," she replied.

"Well, I did, and I sold them to the local news rag...," he paused, his face clouding. "But I didn't realize what it would do to Mei. I've rethought my direction; I think I'll just stick to attending concerts and trying to get the best shots possible of the performers. No more gossip magazine stuff."

"That's more like you anyway, Myles. I'm sure you'll do well," she said, sincerely.

He laughed. "This is a bit of a switch for you, isn't it? You're usually the first one to say 'go for it at all costs' aren't you?"

"I used to be," she sighed.

There was an awkward pause before Myles said, "Well, I'm glad you're okay. I'm going to Katy's now, see ya later!" He bounded down the stairs toward his car; halfway there, he turned to add, "Paula's gone away for a few days. You'll have the place to yourself!"

Lorelei squinted into the bright May sunshine as she watched him drive off. A nice steady lad, she thought. Katy was lucky, though Myles was a bit like David; too what-you-see-is-what-you-get. She liked a bit of mystery in a man. She sighed, thinking of Kwok Lee. Time to go inside and take the first doses of the supplements he had given her.

Under ordinary circumstances, she would welcome the opportunity to have the house to herself, but now she felt sad and unsettled. Many things were going to change, starting with small habits such as the cup of strong tea with something sweet that she always had at this time of day. Kwok Lee had banned caffeine and sugary treats. Instead, she made herself a cup of the herb tea he had given her, and began to open the various bottles of tablets and capsules. There were so many of them, which would have been confusing had Kwok Lee not helpfully attached a label to each bottle on which was written the amount she should take. A few minutes later, she had managed to swallow all of them with copious amounts of the tea, and now she had a nasty aftertaste in her mouth, which she hoped would pass quickly.

Not wanting to store the bottles in the kitchen cupboard and thus be open to her roommates' curiosity, Lorelei went to her room and put them in her dresser. Feeling a little tired, she curled up on her bed with the vegetarian cookbook. Many of the glossy, full-colour photographs did look appetizing, but what on earth was couscous? Or bean curd? She'd start the diet tomorrow; it would be easier as she would be at Kwok Lee's. Yes, tomorrow would be a better day …

Some time later, the shrill ring of the telephone in the kitchen woke her with a start. Lorelei ran to answer it and found that it was her doctor's office, reminding her of the next day's appointment, as she was scheduled to start chemotherapy then. Afraid that she would not make a good job of explaining what she was doing, she simply agreed to be there the next afternoon. She would ask Kwok Lee to go with her.

Her stomach felt empty. Looking at the clock, Lorelei was surprised to discover that she had been asleep for nearly three hours. She retrieved the cookbook and paged through it. No, she would not worry about the diet tonight. Instead, she would gorge herself on things she knew she would not be able to eat for some time. Going to the refrigerator, she found some pork chops; she would have them with mashed potatoes, vegetables with cheese sauce, and ice cream for dessert.

A couple of hours later, after she had eaten and cleaned up, Lorelei, feeling drowsy and bloated, moved to the living room, where she turned the television on and flopped on the couch. She stared at the screen without seeing it, thinking. Damn that Cathi-Ann! She hadn't heard a word from her since that fateful day at the beach. Some friend! Lorelei had to admit that even if Cathi-Ann had called or visited, she wasn't sure if she would have said very much about her experience, or her illness. She was beginning to see that Cathi-Ann was essentially a good-times acquaintance, and not really a friend. Paula had been more of a friend to her, though until very recently, Lorelei hadn't given her much thought.

And then there was Kwok Lee. That he was extremely dedicated to his work, she had no doubt, but he couldn't possibly give everyone the attention he was giving her. Though he seemed to see her for herself, she could not help but think that it was the loss of Lesley that made him so determined to help her. He must have really loved her to have retreated into celibacy as he had. She had never before met such an attractive man who was voluntarily celibate, nor had she known such a thing was possible. To be appreciated for being human, and not just for being a sexually attractive female, was a new experience for her, and paradoxically, rather frustrating. Kwok Lee was so very handsome and mysterious, with an aura of exotic spices and repressed sexuality that would have driven her mad with desire had she not been preoccupied with her health. Tomorrow she would begin the newest chapter of her life, one that she could never have foreseen.

The effort to keep up a brave front drained her of energy. The near death experience had shown her another plane of existence, and if her fate was to die, she did not want it to be a long and drawn out death. Better to go quickly, she thought. What had Kwok Lee said? Something about life itself being a long process of dying, and the important thing was to focus on making a difference in the world through love. She chuckled to herself; she had certainly tried to make a difference, though not in the way that Kwok Lee was thinking.

With some effort, Lorelei got off the couch, switched off the television, and headed for bed. Within a few minutes she was fast asleep. In her slumber, the dragon she had seen in other dreams returned, shining black and gold in the heaven-light. She was not afraid, though it towered over her. Benevolently, the dragon herded her through fields of tall scented plants with strange round pods that she knew the dragon wanted her to eat. It came so close to her that she could see the individual facets of its opalescent eyes, but she still did not eat the pods. It simply watched her as she continued to move through the field, the pods falling to the ground in front of her, making walking difficult. Then she heard the dragon whisper "Please eat," before the dream faded and she slept on.

The next morning, Lorelei awoke with an unusual fear of being alone. She could not understand it; she only knew that she had to get to Kwok Lee's as soon as she could. Quickly she showered and dressed, gulped down a cup of coffee, and made her way to the bus stop where she paced back and forth impatiently until the bus arrived.

Lorelei's anxiety eased once she got off the bus half a block from the shop. Kwok Lee was just giving the student helper his instructions for the day when Lorelei arrived. She went upstairs to wait for him. On the kitchen table, there was a box in which she found a blue ledger and a large sheaf of receipts, which she began to sort into piles. Better to be busy than to have time to fret about things. In a few minutes, Kwok Lee joined her. He was a welcome distraction; she was struck by the quiet vitality he projected, and the way his lips curled in a hint of a smile.

"You don't waste time, do you? Can you make any sense of it?"

"Yes, I think so. What's this say?" she handed him a receipt with an illegible scrawl on it.

"Fifty-two dollars and forty cents for Don Qua capsules. My friend Wong Choi writes in Chinglish!" he laughed.

"And you'll tell me what Don Qua is later," she laughed back. A twinge in her back made her stretch awkwardly.

Kwok Lee was instantly solicitous. "Have you had anything to eat or drink today?" he said, frowning slightly.

"Only coffee." Before he could respond, she continued, "I know, no caffeine starting right now."

He took a chair and pulled it close to her. Taking her hand in his, he looked at it, small and pink against his pale amber skin, and said softly, "Lorelei, you must be serious about this. No halfways, otherwise it won't work." He raised his eyes to hers, eyes that were deep wells of emotion, eyes that Lorelei felt her soul falling into as she trembled at his touch. In other circumstances, she would have gone where her feelings led her, but not now, even though part of her wanted to be distracted from the reality of her illness. Kwok Lee was right; she needed to be committed to her treatment. And besides, Lorelei did not want to face the embarrassment of being refused. Once was enough.

"I'm sorry, Kwok Lee. I did take my tablets."

"That's a good start. Now, I'll make you some breakfast, and then you'll have a massage."

She worked at the accounts while he made the meal. Several times she paused to look at him while he stood at the stove, unaware of her scrutiny. He moved with an unhurried, masculine grace. And she did like a man who could cook, although she was apprehensive about the kinds of foods Kwok Lee wanted her to eat. In a few minutes, he set a steaming bowl in front of her, along with the ubiquitous cleansing tea.

"What's this?"

He laughed. "I have a feeling you will be asking that question many times. It's wet rice with soy milk and a little shredded dried plum."

" 'Wet rice?' "

"Cooked rice that is re-steamed. A very traditional breakfast."

She found it tasted rather like the rice pudding she had been used to in Australia. Perhaps the change in diet wouldn't be so difficult after all. As she ate, she remembered her medical appointment, and asked Kwok Lee if he would accompany her.

"I'm not sure I could explain what we're doing very clearly. And I'm afraid the doctor will shout at me," she said, as she finished eating.

"Yes, doctors tend not to be very receptive to other forms of medicine. Of course I'll go with you." He looked at his watch. "There's enough time for your massage."

Kwok Lee led her downstairs, to a room that led off the back room. Though small, it was tastefully decorated in tones of burgundy, with a thick rug with a geometric pattern on the floor, and a stained glass window high on one wall that let in shades of yellow-orange light. In the middle of the room stood a massage table.

Lorelei looked around, puzzled. "Where do I change?"

"Change?"

"Don't I need to get my gear off in order to have a massage?" She was careful to keep her voice neutral, but in truth, she had been looking forward to this part of her treatment. The prospect of Kwok Lee's long, sensitive fingers touching her body made her shiver in anticipation.

He laughed, but could not quite hide the glint in his eyes. "No, I do reiki massage. You don't need to take your clothes off for that. I use gentle pressure to align your energies. It's an ancient technique."

"Oh," she said, trying to hide her disappointment. Once she was on the table, she was surprised to find that instead of becoming excited as Kwok Lee began to touch her, she relaxed as she began to feel a faint warmth course through her limbs. She felt odd, a little like when she had had the near death experience; if she was somewhere else, aware of nothing but her heartbeat. After a time that could have been an hour or longer, Lorelei startled as Kwok Lee said her name in her ear.

"Oh! I was nearly asleep!" she exclaimed.

"You were in a meditative state. That's good, you're a natural. We'd better get going."

"I'm not looking forward to this…," she looked up at him as she got off the table.

He reached out and touched her arm. "Don't worry, I'll explain everything. That's all we can do."

Lorelei gazed after him as he went into the main shop to speak to the student helper. What was she to him that he would go to this much trouble? Again she thought of the love he had lost. He still grieved for Lesley, she was sure, despite his believing that death was just a transition to another world. Her musings ceased as he returned, car keys in hand.

A short time later, they were being ushered into Dr. Francis' bright and airy office. Without preamble, the middle-aged man launched into a speech about what she could expect during the chemotherapy process. Lorelei tried in vain to interject.

"And your husband here can be there if you like," the doctor seemed to pause for breath. Lorelei seized her chance.

"He's not my husband, he's my…" nerves got the better of her as her mind went blank.

"Naturopath," finished Kwok Lee.

The doctor's bushy eyebrows shot up over his horn-rimmed glasses. "I beg your pardon?" he asked, imperiously.

Kwok Lee began to explain, in detail, the naturopathic treatment of Lorelei's type of cancer, using scientific terms, speaking as an equal. As Kwok Lee spoke, the doctor's jaw set, and his brows furrowed.

"Young man!" he interrupted as Kwok Lee was explaining acid balances, "I do not condone quackery! You are endangering this young woman's life by holding out this fantasy!"

With steely eyes, his voice firm, Kwok Lee replied, "I studied medicine at Oxford before I realized that the narrow parameters of western medicine did not offer the opportunity for healing that traditional Chinese medicine does."

"Be that as it may, you are still offering false hope…"

As the debate had progressed, Lorelei bit her lip to stifle the outburst she felt coming on. Now, with her cheeks flushed, she could no longer keep silent.

Her colour high, her green eyes flashed as she cried, "Kwok Lee's people were practicing medicine when yours were still living in caves!"

The two men fell silent as Lorelei blinked in surprise. She recovered quickly as she continued, "My mind is made up. Thank you, Dr. Francis. Come on, Kwok Lee." She stood and headed for the door. Kwok

Lee smiled widely as he, too, stood.

"You'll regret this, young lady. Mark my words," said the doctor as they left.

Once they were outside in the street, Kwok Lee turned to her and said, "You were magnificent in there!" His eyes shone with admiration.

Delicious warmth played its way through Lorelei's body, settling in her breasts and loins as she absorbed his reaction to her outburst. She looked away in embarrassment before she answered him. "Well, he was such a narrow-minded dickhead!" Suddenly debilitated, she swayed, and nearly fainted before Kwok Lee caught her.

"I was afraid of this," he said. "You've managed to wear yourself out. When we get back to my place, you're having a nap."

Though she had planned on running a few errands, including paying a visit to the art gallery where she had almost forgotten she had some works on exhibit, she was too fatigued to protest. Meekly she allowed Kwok Lee to help her into his vehicle, and on the way home she was only too conscious of the worried glances he cast her way. It seemed to be a very long time before she was finally ensconced in Kwok Lee's own large bed; gratefully she allowed herself to slide into the haven of sleep.

Some time later, the smell of food cooking penetrated Lorelei's consciousness. For a moment, she did not know where she was. The shadows on the wall opposite told her that it was late in the day, long past suppertime, given how long the days were in May. The room spun around her as she sat up; she grabbed the side of the bed until the dizziness subsided. Her head was throbbing, and her bones ached. She looked around the room. The large bed was covered with an ultramarine-blue silk bedspread on which was embroidered a gold and black dragon, not unlike the one of her dreams. The furniture was of carved mahogany, and a large sandalwood trunk stood in one corner. A large lacquer-framed mirror hung on the wall, along with delicate painted panels of silk. The walls were papered with a subtle green pattern of bamboo reeds. He really had exquisite taste, she thought.

Lorelei made her way, somewhat shakily, into the kitchen, where she found Kwok Lee busily labouring over a hot wok. He looked up as she entered. "You must be hungry," he said. "I know you haven't had anything since breakfast, not even water, and you ought to be drinking lots of that."

"One thing at a time," she replied, rather grumpily. "Oh, my head is pounding and why do I ache all over?"

"That'll be caffeine withdrawal," he said, spooning food into two large, wide bowls. "It'll last a week or so. People don't realize that their daily coffee or tea is addictive."

"I do now; I'd kill for a coffee or a good cup of tea," she said gloomily, as he placed a bowl of steaming food in front of her. "Cack! What is this muck? The only things I recognize are the carrots."

"You are being very Australian, not recognizing any food that isn't dripping with blood," he teased, as he set large glasses of water on the table.

"You could talk!" she retorted. "You're just a pommy bastard with a tan!"

He laughed. "Nice try, but you won't distract me. This is bean curd, sui choy, and carrots with brown rice in a light plum sauce, with a little daikon radish as a garnish. Eat it up, now."

"I don't feel hungry," she said, petulantly.

"That's exactly why you should eat," he said quietly, sitting in the chair opposite.

His voice held so much concern for her. Lorelei looked into his eyes, saw the fear lurking there. How could she refuse him? She picked up her fork and began eating, tentatively at first, but as she tasted the delicate flavour of the food, she began to eat with relish.

Kwok Lee noticed, and said, "See, it's not so bad. You will have to be prepared for your body to protest the new diet."

"How do you mean?" asked Lorelei, her fork in midair.

"Your system has been used to a certain kind of food, and it will need to adjust to the change. You will feel very hungry soon after eating a meal like this, but with time, that reaction will cease."

"Oh I hope so," she replied. "I like being a carnivore; I've always loved the feel of meat in my mouth." As soon as the words were spoken, Lorelei's face flushed to the roots of her hair. "Oh, oh...I'm...I didn't mean...I'm sorry..."

Kwok Lee's clear, musical laugh filled the air. He regarded her in an amused fashion as he said, "Just because I'm celibate doesn't mean I don't enjoy a risqué comment." He paused slightly before continuing earnestly, "I do know what sex is like."

The conversation was drifting into an area neither of them was comfortable with. Feeling self-conscious, Lorelei applied herself to her food until the bowl was empty, while Kwok Lee did the same. When she was done, she said, "Thank you for the dinner, Kwok Lee." She stood and began to clear the table of dirty dishes.

"No, Lorelei. You just sit. I'll put these away."

She had no choice but to watch him as he made fast work of washing the dishes and cleaning up. When he was done, he turned to her as she began yawning. "Hmm, I think I better take you home so you can get some rest."

It was dark as Kwok Lee drove through the unusually quiet streets of Tillicum. Clouds had rolled in off the sea, and a light misty rain was falling, keeping young, late-spring revellers indoors. Had it not been for her present circumstances, Lorelei would have been one of them. She was almost asleep as Kwok Lee pulled the truck to the curb in front of her home.

"Thank you, Kwok Lee, thank you for everything," she said, softly. "I don't know what I would have done had I not met you."

In the dark, she couldn't read his expression as he said, "The fates have a way of putting things you need in your path. You only have to recognize them."

There was no reply to such a deep statement. After a moment, she said, "Thank you again. Do you need me to work tomorrow?"

He told her that since she had made such good headway in the paperwork, she only needed to see him for the daily massage. She promised to come to him the next morning, and bid him goodnight.

The house was empty when she entered, but there was a note beside the phone from Myles saying that her lawyer had called. What could it mean? Would she be officially divorced soon? Or was David going to make things difficult? Fortunately, she was so exhausted that she could not stay awake to ponder the possibility.

– Chapter Ten –

An incessant banging on the front door woke Lorelei out of a sound sleep the next morning. With difficulty, she got out of bed and stumbled dizzily through the living room. Her head felt stuffed with cotton wool. Opening the door, she blinked in surprise as she saw Cathi-Ann, who was carrying a rectangular, plastic-wrapped package. Lorelei didn't want company, but could not summon the energy to send Cathi-Ann on her way. Feeling faint, she merely muttered, "Come in," and ran quickly back to her bed and pulled the covers up to her chin, while Cathi-Ann followed.

Her friend sat at the end of the bed, and looked away for a few seconds before taking a deep breath. Her words came out in a hurry, as if she was afraid she would lose the ability to speak. "Oh, Lore, I'm sorry I didn't come to see you in the hospital. I know I should have…"

Lorelei cut her off. "Bloody right! They said they didn't know why I was still alive." She was reluctant to tell Cathi-Ann about her near death experience, as she doubted that Cathi-Ann would be comfortable with such an esoteric subject, and she feared the ridicule that was sure to follow should she divulge her experience to her.

"It's just that, jeez, I can't handle stuff like that!"

"So I noticed," Lorelei said, rather coldly.

Cathi-Ann regarded her earnestly. "C'mon, I said I was sorry! And why are you in bed at this time on a Tuesday morning?"

Sighing, Lorelei chose her words carefully. She did not want to give any hint of her illness, did not want to seem to be demanding an unusual amount of attention from her free-spirited friend. "Oh, I'm just tired, and I think I'm coming down with something," she said, as she remembered that she needed to call her lawyer. "But I do need to get up and go do some things today."

"Wanna hang out?" Cathi-Ann asked, hopefully.

Lorelei, though beginning to forgive her friend for being absent after her recent trials, was not in a mood for Cathi-Ann's somewhat strident personality. "No, I have too many errands to run, and I think I'll be all worn out by the time I'm finished," she said.

"Oh." Cathi-Ann had clearly not been expecting to be rebuffed. She brightened as she continued, "Well, then, do you wanna go to the bar one Friday? Steve's fishing every weekend for the next three weeks. We can see if we can get ourselves kicked out again, and who knows what else?" She waggled her eyebrows at Lorelei, the implications clear.

"Maybe, I'll see how things go," Lorelei said, knowing that if she refused outright, Cathi-Ann would suspect that something was wrong, or be worried that Lorelei was more angry with her than she let on. "What's that?" she asked, indicating the package Cathi-Ann had set on the floor.

"Your prints that were in the exhibit, the ones that didn't sell. Samantha Meadows asked if I could bring these to you as you hadn't been there in a long time," Cathi-Ann answered. Shifting to a more comfortable position at the end of the bed, she launched into a long story about what some mutual acquaintances had done the previous weekend. "Anyway, it was a real good party," Cathi-Ann finished.

Lorelei had only been half-listening as she wondered how she could get Cathi-Ann to leave without hurting her feelings, and did not realize that she had finished telling her story.

"Lore? You weren't even listening!" protested the dark-haired girl.

"Sorry," Lorelei mumbled. "Have to see my lawyer today."

"Okay, okay, I'll get going then. Call me later in the week. See you."

Lorelei waited until she heard the slam of the front door as her friend left, then she got out of bed. Although she still felt faint, she forced herself to drink some herb tea and eat a little fruit for breakfast. She did not forget to take the supplements Kwok Lee had given her, though she still disliked the strange aftertaste.

Still in her pajamas, Lorelei called her lawyer's office, and was astounded to be told that David had proposed a lump sum payment to her, and if she agreed, all she needed to do is sign some papers and then they would be divorced. Though she could have continued to contest the division of assets, Lorelei was elated; soon she would be free of David forever.

She showered and dressed quickly. Though she still felt unwell, the feeling was superceded by the prospect of David no longer being in her life, and having enough money to not have to worry about bills for a while. Just before she left, the phone rang. It was her employer at the group home, asking if she could work that evening. Though she had her doubts about whether her energy level would be equal to the task, she accepted the shift.

Within the hour, she had visited her lawyer's office and completed the necessary paperwork; it was only a matter of time before she would receive David's cheque. She felt almost giddy as she made her way to Kwok Lee's. When she entered the shop, Lorelei could hardly contain her excitement as she waited for Kwok Lee to finish serving a customer.

Once the woman had left, Kwok Lee said, "Well, tell me! I can see you're bursting with some sort of news."

Lorelei couldn't get the words out fast enough.

As he replaced stock on the bottom shelves, he listened, then said, "Oh, but that's marvellous! You don't need to worry about finances so much." He smiled, looking genuinely pleased for her.

"Yeah, but I'm still going to work; in fact I have to work tonight," she said, daring him to challenge her.

"Mmm, only you will know when you're doing too much," he said, standing to reach the upper shelves.

"Ohh, you are infuriating sometimes!" Lorelei exclaimed, only half-serious. She left the room and went upstairs, where she knew there would be some book work waiting. Lorelei simply could not understand Kwok Lee when he did not react to her as other men did. She had expected him to order her not to work, but instead he had merely accepted the fact. If he really was so concerned about her health, shouldn't he have protested? And yet, she couldn't deny the empathy and nurturing she had received from him. He really was an enigma sometimes.

By Friday, Lorelei's days had settled into a pattern; she would arrive at the shop each morning, when Kwok Lee would ask her many questions regarding her diet and how she was feeling. Then, she would have her reiki massage, which she enjoyed immensely, it being the only time Kwok Lee ever touched her. It was also the only part of her day when she felt completely relaxed and at peace. After the massage, she would work on Kwok Lee's accounts, and if she did not need to do that, she ran errands. The work at the group home proved to be less taxing than she had feared, though she always rested before she reported for duty.

With the exception of breakfast, which she always had at home, Kwok Lee prepared all her meals. Seeing the effort he was putting into each meal to make sure she was getting the nutrition she needed, Lorelei was careful not to complain. The truth was she was finding it difficult to adjust to a meatless diet where a typical meal might consist of brown rice, steamed parsnips, and asparagus, along with fresh blueberry juice, and the ubiquitous supplements. And what was the point? She felt terrible most of the time. The headaches persisted, along with a general irritability that she struggled to keep hidden.

Always one who liked her independence, she was beginning to find Kwok Lee's constant solicitousness annoying. For nearly three weeks she said nothing; spending each night in her own bed helped to dispel her rising frustration, though she was lonely, having given up socializing. She seldom saw her roommates as they went on with their full schedules. On a Friday afternoon in June, Kwok Lee was trying to persuade her to meditate with him, as he did every day; she found she could contain herself no longer.

"I don't want to fucking meditate! Keep your airy-fairy crap to yourself! I can't do this anymore! You're always following me, always watching every bite I eat! Just leave me alone!" She stood facing him, hands on her hips, eyes flashing, daring him to argue with her.

He flinched slightly, but did not seem very surprised at her outburst. Taking a deep breath, and looking thoughtful, he said quietly, "This is just your fear talking, Lorelei. Your fear of the disease, fear of your life changing, your fear of the unknown. It's good that it's come out."

"Screw you!" she cried. "Screw you and your emotionally expressive all natural crap!"

His voice still quiet and gentle, Kwok Lee replied, "I just want you to have the best care possible…"

"Why?" she spat the word, as she moved closer for the final blow. "So you can feel less guilty about Lesley?" she sneered. His face blanched as she continued, "I'm not her! I'm me! And maybe I *want* to die…" With hot tears streaming down her face, she ran out of the shop, slamming the door behind her, setting in motion events that would have dire consequences.

When she reached home, she was glad that her roommates were out. Thoughts that she had been keeping buried for the past several weeks came to the surface of her mind. That Kwok Lee! He was only using her to assuage his own guilty conscience. Though she had had moments when she had believed that he appreciated her for herself, she now dismissed those times as delusions. Every time he looked at her, he saw Lesley. How was she to compete with a dead woman? He had cut himself off from the possibility of happiness with someone else, while enjoying her attraction to him, using her illness as an excuse to keep her close by. She'd show him! After today, she would go back to her doctor, and ask for the standard treatment. For now, she felt like getting blindingly drunk. Remembering Cathi-Ann's suggestion, she called her friend, who was only too eager to meet at the same bar they had gone to before.

Lorelei prepared for the evening with all the instincts of a black widow spider going hunting for a mate. She dressed the part in a long-sleeved, form-fitting black mini-dress with a plunging neckline, black pantyhose and black stilettos with shiny silver heels. With her eyes heavily made up with green eyeshadow, and dark plum-coloured lipstick, and her terra-cotta hair falling loosely past her shoulders, no one was going to fail to notice her tonight. When she got to the bar, she found Cathi-Ann waiting for her outside.

"Jeez, you're loaded for bear tonight! I'm like a rag bag compared to you," laughed Cathi-Ann, indicating the long floral-print skirt and loose white chemise she wore. "Are you hoping that guy you danced with is here, whatsisname, Blackie?"

"Well, maybe," Lorelei replied, slyly.

"You just better make sure the girlfriend isn't here. I don't wanna get thrown out again!"

"Oh, come on, you liked the excitement," teased Lorelei. Cathi-Ann simply shot her a glance that confirmed Lorelei's statement as they made their way inside the dark establishment where a country-western band was getting ready to play. It was early, with few people seated at the tables that surrounded the dance floor, and a cluster of people at the bar. Cathi-Ann ordered the drinks and did not seem to notice that Lorelei's attention was elsewhere as she began one of her long-winded stories. Making quick work of her drink, Lorelei ordered another as she kept her eyes on the bar. She thought she saw…yes, it was Blackie, dressed much the same as he had been before, in jeans, leather vest and cowboy boots, his long, shaggy hair framing his unshaven face.

Suddenly, Cathi-Ann stopped talking. "You're doing it again, not listening! What is it? Is he here?"

"Yeah, but I haven't had enough to drink yet," replied Lorelei, a fiercely determined glint in her eyes.

"Well, just remember what happened before. Make sure he's alone this time," said Cathi-Ann. "You want another?" she asked, nodding at the half-empty glass in Lorelei's hand.

Lorelei gulped down the rest of her drink and said, "Yeah, make it another double."

As the band began their first set, Lorelei made short work of her drink and ordered another, while Cathi-Ann tapped her feet to the music. Soon, a man had pulled her onto the dance floor, leaving Lorelei alone. Having downed her third drink, Lorelei got up and made her way across the room, to where Blackie leaned against the bar, laughing with a couple of other equally-scruffy men, who fell silent as she approached. Lorelei came up behind him and tapped his back. He turned around.

"Little Red!" he said, his face lighting up. "I hoped you'd come back. Wanna dance?" he said, glancing at his companions, who grinned lecherously. The band was starting to play a slow, romantic song. Lorelei showed her teeth in her most enticing smile and let him take her hand and lead her to the dance floor. He pulled her close and said in her ear, "Don't worry, Little Red. My girlfriend's gone out of town for a few days. We can do whatever we want." He rubbed his groin suggestively against her abdomen. This time she did not recoil. She leaned into him, pressing her breasts against him as they danced. The song ended, but he did not let her go. "Let's get out of here," he said. "I don't live too far away."

Lorelei glanced across the dance floor, where Cathi-Ann was sitting with three other people whom she obviously knew. "Let's go," she said, a hard, determined note in her voice. Blackie led her out a side door, the same door through which she and Cathi-Ann had been thrown out a couple of months before. A light rain was beginning to fall as Lorelei struggled to keep up with him in her high heels. He continued down the street half a block and turned into a door that led up a flight of steep, narrow stairs, and into a dimly lit, dank hallway. The smell of urine, stale cigarette smoke, and beer hung in the air like a foul miasma.

In a moment, Blackie had unlocked the door to his apartment, and switched on the light, revealing a room with paint of an indeterminable colour peeling off the walls, and large stains on the ceiling. A chenille bedspread seemed to be trying in vain to cover a threadbare couch while an old console style television with a bent hanger for an antenna stood depressively in a corner. Fragments of fossilized pizza littered a wooden cable spool that served as a coffee table. Liquor bottles and overflowing ashtrays covered every available surface. Blackie wasted no time as he headed for the bedroom, shedding clothes as he went, while Lorelei, in her high heels, delicately picked her way through the debris on the floor.

"Don't be shy, baby, c'mere!" Blackie called from the bedroom. A loud belch followed this demand. He was already in the bed grinning in anticipation. Lorelei could see his erection under the faded yellow sheet that was the only covering on the bed. With the air of a woman about to perform a distasteful, yet necessary chore, she shed her clothes quickly and scuttled under the sheet, ignoring the strong smell of perspiration that emanated from Blackie's body.

He was immediately on top of her, lips and tongue slobbering her face like an ecstatic dog, rough, ape-like hands pawing her breasts, and a face like sandpaper against her alabaster skin. She flinched as she felt his teeth on her tender flesh. An image of Kwok Lee's handsome face flashed in her mind; she pushed it away as she positioned herself for Blackie to enter her. He eagerly did so, clumsily shoving herself inside her with no regard for her comfort. Lorelei almost revelled in the pain as he thrust harder and harder inside her.

"Make some noise," he growled in her ear. She obliged with a performance worthy of an Oscar winning actress. He shuddered as he reached climax, and as soon as he did, he slid off and out of her, leaving his ejaculate to spew out of her like the pustulous secretion of a putrid disease. This was what men were really like, thought Lorelei. I'm drunk and I don't care. Screw Kwok Lee and his I'm-meant-to-be-a-healer crap. Screw David and his money. If I die I won't be missing anything.

"Aha! You again!" the shrill voice startled her into sitting up, fully sober now, revealing for a moment angry red bite marks on her full breasts. It was Blackie's girlfriend!

Blackie leaped out of the bed, pulling the sheet with him. "Terrie, honey, she's nothing…"

The stringy blonde woman pulled Lorelei off the bed, and dragged her naked through the apartment, screaming for her clothes. The woman, though thin, was wiry, and Lorelei was no match for her, drunk as she was.

"You little bitch! I told you to stay away from my man!" Terrie hissed at her as she dragged her down the stairs and down a back hallway. Lorelei was still screaming, but in this area of Tillicum, with its rough bars and strip clubs, no one would think anything was amiss. Terrie kicked a door open and threw her bodily out into the alley, where she landed in a large puddle.

Stunned, Lorelei lay silent for a moment, the rain beating down on her, before she cautiously staggered to her feet. She had to find shelter. Hoping no one would see her, she kept to the shadows as she made her hesitant way in her bare feet down the narrow, dark alley. She froze as something moved in the shadows off to her right; terrified of rats, Lorelei stood holding her breath as a small shadow came out from behind a garbage bin and crossed a small patch of light ahead of her. She gasped in relief as she realized it was only an old tomcat. Oh God, what was she to do? How could she have gone with Blackie? She could hardly go knocking on doors for help, stark naked as she was. And who would miss her? Certainly not Cathi-Ann, who would only assume that she had gone off to have some fun. Lorelei shuddered as an image of herself and Blackie rutting like wild animals came to mind. With an urgency borne of her self-loathing, she stepped under a torrent of water that fell from a leaky gutter; if she died out here, she would at least be clean.

Soaking wet and shivering, Lorelei backed against a wall that offered little shelter as a feeling of despair enveloped her as her small body began to tremble with silent, heaving sobs. What was that? Footsteps? She held her breath, and scrunched down to make herself smaller as she tried to see who was approaching. It would be just her luck to get attacked after what had happened tonight. Two people were in the darkness beyond the large dumpster ahead. She shifted position; as she did so, she let out an involuntary grunt.

"Someone's out there!" said a female voice, somehow familiar.

"Who's there?" called a male voice, a voice she knew as well as her own. Lorelei wanted to run toward him, but in her nakedness, she hesitated. "Kwok Lee!" she sobbed. "Kwok Lee!" As she heard Kwok Lee and his companion move rapidly toward her, she rose and stumbled towards them.

"Oh my God, she's naked!"

"Paula!" Lorelei cried, as the tall woman pulled off her jacket and wrapped it around her.

Kwok Lee said nothing, but swept her up in his arms; she was only too glad to snuggle into him, as she had done before. "I'm sorry, I'm sorry," she mumbled, between sobs. Once again, Kwok Lee had been there to rescue her, unbidden, just when she needed him.

"Easy, easy. Don't speak, you're safe now. Let's get you home first." His gentle voice held no resentment, only warm reassurance…and something else that made her heart soar. It had taken some time, but she now knew; in his arms, she was home.

— Chapter Eleven —

Kwok Lee bundled Lorelei into the back seat of Paula's car and got in with her.

Though her crying had subsided with the relief of being found, she was shivering and barely aware of the short, urgent exchange between her friends.

"We should take her home," said Paula.

"No," said Kwok Lee, rather sharply. "I'm closer; we can help her sooner if we go there."

"Maybe we should go to the police. Anything could have happened."

"No, there's no reason to do that!" cried Lorelei. Kwok Lee's arms tightened around her as he said softly in her ear, "I know," and, raising his voice, said to Paula, "Let's just get to my place."

Lorelei gratefully sank into Kwok Lee's arms. Silently contrite, she pondered her actions. How could she have gone with Blackie? The alcohol wasn't to blame; she had known full well what she was doing. She did not know how Kwok Lee and Paula had known where to find her, but it was clear they had both been worried about her.

A few minutes later, Paula had parked the car behind the shop, and had gone ahead of them with the keys to unlock the doors, while Kwok Lee followed, carrying Lorelei up the stairs and directly to his bedroom. He gently deposited her on the bed, then left the room to run a hot bath for her while Lorelei returned Paula's jacket and wrapped the sheets around her naked body. When the bath was ready,

Lorelei found that Kwok Lee had poured scented oil into it; with joy she lowered her body into the steaming water. After a good long soak during which she scrubbed her body until her skin glowed pink, Lorelei returned to the bed, wrapped in one of Kwok Lee's robes. It was only then that she was able to speak coherently. Paula sat on the edge of the bed while Kwok Lee hovered close by.

"What happened? Were you attacked?" asked Paula.

"No, no, nothing like that," sniffed Lorelei. She was silent as she contemplated what she wanted to say. Taking a deep breath, she said, "I'm sorry. I was angry when I left you this afternoon, Kwok Lee. And you've only been trying to help me get better."

"But I don't understand," said Paula. "What is it?" she said, as Lorelei and Kwok Lee exchanged glances.

"I have cancer," Lorelei whispered, as if the words were shards of glass.

Paula's eyes grew large as she said, "Oh, Lorelei! And you never said a word!"

"I didn't want to bother anyone. There was the divorce, and everyone's busy with their own lives…and some people don't seem to care at all," Lorelei said, remembering Cathi-Ann.

"Including yourself," Paula said, softly.

Lorelei said nothing, as her perceptive friend's comment struck a chord within her.

"I think I'll go make some tea while you girls talk," said Kwok Lee.

"Ginger tea?" asked Lorelei, her voice that of a little girl.

"Of course," he replied, flashing a reassuring smile as he closed the bedroom door behind him.

Lorelei fiddled with the coverlet before looking into Paula's eyes. Seeing only empathy and acceptance there, she said, "You're right, Paula. I'm not very self-aware am I? How did you find me?"

Paula had gone with a date to the bar, unusual for her, but the man she'd been with sometimes enjoyed going there. After half an hour, she had encountered Cathi-Ann, who told her that Lorelei had left with Blackie.

"And I got a shiver up my spine when she told me that, Lorelei. I knew something was wrong. Cathi-Ann couldn't understand why I wanted to go looking for you, so I left and went to Kwok Lee's."

"Why didn't your date go with you?"

"He couldn't understand the urgency any more than Cathi-Ann could. I left him happily enjoying a drink with her. Kwok Lee was just leaving as I got here. He had been meditating…and he saw you."

A cold wind of mortification swept through Lorelei's being. Though she had tried to push them aside, she now had no doubt of Kwok Lee's abilities. He had seen her with Blackie, had seen them together. Her eyes downcast, she continued to twist the edge of the coverlet in her hands for a moment before raising her eyes to Paula's, whispering, "Then...you know what I was doing."

"Actually, Kwok Lee didn't say, but I could see he was worried. You...you don't have to tell me if you don't want to...Lorelei, I think he really loves you...though maybe he doesn't know it yet."

Before she could reply, he was back, bearing a tray, which he set on the bedside table.

"You've been treating Lorelei for her cancer?" asked Paula.

"Yes," he said, pouring a cup of tea and handing to Lorelei, who sipped it gratefully. He passed another cup to Paula. "Complete diet detox, reiki, and supplements."

"Only I haven't helped...I didn't pay attention. You said I'd feel ill as the treatment began to work, and when that turned out to be true, I couldn't face it. I just assumed it was all in vain, and I was going to die anyway. I wanted to live on the edge, to feel excitement and danger... so I ran off with Carl...and even when I drowned I tried hard not to think about what it all meant...and then tonight...what must you think of me, Kwok Lee..." she broke off, unable to say more.

Kwok Lee sat on the opposite side of the bed to Paula. His voice gentle, he said, "That you've been very afraid, and confused, and rather full of self-loathing..."

"And acting like I'm possessed..."

"Well, in a way, you are. Cancer can possess you..."

"And denial is very common when people are diagnosed; it's such a shock," said Paula.

"And now, I've wasted time. What if it's too late?"

"We try harder," said Kwok Lee. "I've an idea. I think you should move in with me so I can keep an eye on you."

"Move in? Where...where..."

"There's a small spare room at the end of the hall."

"Maybe it's a good thing, Lore," Paula said. "Myles and Katy are moving in together, and I'm going to ditch my stuff with my parents and go travelling. If you're here you won't have to worry about getting new roommates. Why don't I go back to the house now and get some of your things?"

Lorelei looked at Kwok Lee, who smiled and nodded encouragement. For the first time in a long while, she felt hopeful. Here she was, as low as she had ever been, yet here were two people who were willing to put themselves out for her, who were worried about her, who dropped what they were doing to help her. "Yes, yes, please do," she said. Her trembling voice betrayed her emotion as she continued, "and….thank you…both of you."

"The only thing that matters is that you get better," said Paula, patting her arm. "Now, I will leave you in Kwok Lee's capable hands. I'll be back in a while."

After she had left, Lorelei sighed and said, "I suppose I should get some rest, but I want to talk first. I'm sorry, Kwok Lee, I said some terrible things…"

He sat on the edge of the bed before he answered. "Perhaps necessary things. I have tried to hang on to Lesley…I told you that she used to come to me when I meditated. She hasn't done so for a long time now, though I have tried many times to see her. The last time she came to me, she said that there would be another…but I did not want to hear it. You said you hadn't been self aware, but I don't think I've been either. I have been hanging on to my grief and guilt." His voice full of emotion, he continued, "Maybe I did see you as a second Lesley…just in the beginning…but I now see that you are even more dynamic," he smiled slightly. "When I met you, you scared me. I believed that I was not meant to be with anyone but Lesley; and I'd lived like that for a long time."

Lorelei felt her heart flutter as she realized what he was saying. Paula was right, he did love her! After the heartbreak of losing Lesley, after believing he would never love another, he had been surprised and frightened by his attraction to her. Bravely, she asked, "And now?"

"I see a wonderful, lovely possibility here in front of me. But we have to get you well first." As he looked earnestly into her eyes, she felt herself enveloped in his aura; warm, safe, and protected.

Lorelei sat up, and wrapped her arms around her knees, being careful to keep the blankets wrapped around her. "Kwok Lee, you're so different from other men that I've known. I expected you to forbid me to work after I started treatment, but you didn't."

"Is the butterfly more beautiful when you hold it captive in your hands or when you see it hovering free above a field of wildflowers? You needed to find your way on your own."

"But look what I did…I deliberately slept with someone I didn't know…or like." The words came out in a rush as she described meeting Blackie and going back to his apartment. "And…and you saw me!" In shame, she buried her face in her hands.

Kwok Lee gently patted her shoulder. "Yes, and I hold no judgment of you. You were hurting and knew no other way to express it. I believe I was meant to see you…its part of my, of our, healing."

"Oh, Kwok Lee!" she cried as he embraced her. She pulled away from him. Looking deeply into eyes, eyes that pierced her very soul, she said, "I promise, I'll heed all your instructions. I want to get better. I…I haven't believed it was possible and…I think somewhere I decided to hasten my departure from this life. The near death experience showed me a place where there was no pain, and I wanted so much to be there, but it's not time…I have things to do before I go back there."

"I'm so glad to hear you say these things, Lorelei. It means you are really on the path to healing," he said, stroking her cheek.

She leaned into his touch, and sighed contentedly. "I think I'd like to have a rest now."

She slept for an hour or so, until Paula had delivered her things, which Kwok Lee placed in his bedroom, telling her that the room was hers until she could move her own furniture into the spare room. Exhausted, and feeling blissfully secure, she sank again beneath the warm covers of Kwok Lee's bed and almost instantly, fell asleep.

— Chapter Twelve —

Several weeks went by during which Lorelei held true to her word about following Kwok Lee's instructions. He made it easier for her by taking time from his thriving business to help her with her meals, and give her reiki massage each morning. He continued to be solicitous while managing to give her enough space that she did not feel pressured or crowded.

When she received the money she had been expecting from David, she decided that she no longer needed the job at the group home, which was just as well. The organization that ran the home had undergone restructuring with the result that the home was now admitting clients with far more challenging issues than Lorelei was comfortable working with, which created stress she did not need. Kwok Lee supported her, but did not try to influence her decision.

One day, she realized that her back no longer ached, her digestive and monthly troubles had all but disappeared, and her abdomen no longer felt heavy and bloated. For the first time in a long time, she felt full of energy. She said as much to Kwok Lee over breakfast one sunny morning.

"I reckon I should go back to the doctor and get a check-up, don't you?" she said, mischievously.

Kwok Lee smiled as he asked, "Would you like me to go with you again?"

"Mmm, better not," she replied, as she tucked into the platter of fresh fruit slices that he had just placed in front of her. "Dr. Francis was nearly exploded when he met you; I shudder to think what his reaction would be now. Besides," she said coyly, "Do you want him to mistake you for my husband again?"

"That was the only good thing that happened last time!" he exclaimed.

Lorelei was suddenly conscious of a long-absent yearning deep inside her. Though Kwok Lee had never lost his attraction for her, but over the days and weeks of her treatment, she had concentrated on making her body healthy again. Always aware that Kwok Lee, too, was healing, she had been very careful to avoid suggestive remarks or behaviour, though she had not given up her love of flattering, slightly provocative clothing. How unlike the take-no-prisoners Lorelei that her rambunctious art student friends knew. If they could see her now, they would think she'd had a personality transplant. Almost without realizing it, she giggled.

"It's nice to hear you laugh," said Kwok Lee. "Care to let me in on the joke?"

Still coy, she said, "Another time."

In the same vein, he replied, "I'll look forward to that."

Such flirting between them was a daily occurrence, one that Lorelei enjoyed immensely, as it was evidence of their mutual attraction, though sometimes she was impatient for him to make a move. At such times she reassured herself that when the time was right, both of them would know it.

In the evenings, they took long walks hand in hand on the boardwalk that ran along Tillicum's waterfront. While she had been ill, Lorelei had been barely aware of the passing summer season, since she had not been out anywhere since she had gone on the ill-fated trip to Jingle Shell Beach with Cathi-Ann. A few days later, after she had had her medical check-up, they were taking their usual walk as Lorelei described the doctor's reaction to finding that all her tests were clear.

"His eyebrows were writhing about on his forehead like confused caterpillars, and if his lower lip had stuck out any further, you could have used it for a bookshelf! I think he was disappointed that I hadn't died after refusing chemotherapy!" she exclaimed, indignant.

Kwok Lee's hand gripped hers tighter as he said, "Let him be disappointed. We don't care what he thinks, do we? The important thing is that you are well."

Lorelei leaned against him as he put his arm around her. How wonderful to have someone really care about her! Sighing contentedly, she looked out over the water toward the setting sun. She had forgotten how she loved the colours of the sky at this time of day, with its deep orange-reds, streaks of magenta, and the faint flash of bright green as the sun sank into the sea. Flocks of birds headed for their night sanctuaries flew low over the lapping waves while a seal paddled close to shore, disappearing below the surface in its hunt for succulent oysters.

"Oh Kwok Lee, I forgot how beautiful the world can be!"

"I'm glad you said that," he said, pausing before he continued. "You know, I've never seen any of your artwork…"

She reflected a moment before replying. "You know how to read me, don't you? I was just thinking that it was time I got back into my printmaking. While I was ill, I became distant from it… I'm not one who can use my art to explore pain when I'm going through it… but afterwards, when I feel better about things, that's when my creativity flows."

"Hmmm. Well, you know I own the building I'm in…"

"Yes?" she asked, wondering what he was getting at.

"There's empty space that you can use for a studio. Needs a little fitting up, but it should do."

With new creative opportunities ahead, Lorelei could hardly wait to begin the task of turning the large space that was currently being used for storage into a studio, while Kwok Lee called upon friends in various trades to do the remodelling. Many days went by in a flurry of shelf and cupboard building, the installation of a ventilation system, and painting and plumbing. When it was finished, the space consisted of a small gallery that opened onto the street, and a large studio outfitted with the latest printmaking equipment.

After the last of the workmen had left, Lorelei stood in wonderment in the centre of the studio, just looking around. Now that she had David's money, she had offered to pay for the remodeling herself, but Kwok Lee had only allowed her to buy the paint. He must love her if he had done all this for her! She would be able to produce some really marvelous work now that she had this bright and airy studio, and she would not have to worry about art galleries taking a percentage of her sales with her own little gallery, which she had named Vivid Imaginings. So lost in thought was she that Lorelei did not hear Kwok Lee enter the room. She jumped as she turned around and found him standing right behind her, an amused expression on his face.

"Happy?" he asked.

"Oh, yes! It's everything I could want!" Her voice trembled with gratitude as she whispered, "Thank you."

"Thank *you*," he said. Stepping closer, he took a lock of her hair and twirled it around his finger in what she realized was a gesture of extreme affection, if not love. How handsome he looked, dressed as he was in a black, long sleeved mandarin shirt that set off his broad shoulders, and snug-fitting jeans that emphasized his narrow hips. He stood so close that she could detect the scent of lemongrass mingled with something else; a musky, masculine fragrance that set her heart racing. She ached for him, yet she knew now was not the moment; she would need to be patient for a little while longer.

With the studio finished, the only thing left to do was to buy supplies, which Lorelei set out to do one afternoon when Kwok Lee was busy with customers. Just outside the art supply store, Lorelei encountered Mei Lundgren, who, with eyes downcast, did not see her at first.

"Oh, hi, Lorelei. Sorry, I was thinking of something else."

"Hi. How are things? Last I heard you were with Michael Allison."

Mei seemed to hide beneath her waist-length dark hair as she explained that Michael had wanted her to travel on tour with him, but she did not care for his partying lifestyle, which would not allow her to pursue her own interests. "I thought it was real, but it wasn't," she finished, her large brown eyes bright with unshed tears.

Lorelei almost wept herself, feeling the pain and longing of her doe-eyed friend. Such a deep sense of empathy for another had rarely occurred before her near death experience, before Kwok Lee had made her aware of things she had never had any knowledge of; and for Lorelei, it was a humbling, yet welcome feeling. She reached out and patted Mei's arm kindly and said, "If it ever was, he'll be back."

Mei sighed, and said, "I don't know. How about you? Are you seeing anyone?"

"In a way," said Lorelei, "do you know Kwok Lee Morgan?"

"I know who he is...he's very good-looking."

"He's been helping me overcome some health problems," said Lorelei. She went on to describe how he had been a gentle, yet steady presence in her life, and how it had become apparent to her that he had very deep feelings for her. "Oh that's nice," said Mei. "It sounds like he'd be very good for you, being in the field he's in. Unlike musicians, he would probably make a nice boyfriend."

"What do you mean?"

"Sorry, baby, we gotta practice; sorry baby, we gotta gig; that girl meant nothing to me, baby, I love you..."

"I see your point," said Lorelei.

"Anyway, good luck with him. Better run now," Mei said, as she moved off.

Lorelei watched her go, thinking about what she had said. That Mei had had her heart broken was obvious, but Lorelei had detected no regret in the other girl's voice, just the pain of love won and lost. What Mei had said about Kwok Lee being very good for her rang in her ears, and made her resolve to continue to be patient, no matter how intense her desire for Kwok Lee became.

After she bought her supplies, Lorelei was on her way home, laden with her purchases, when she turned a corner and almost ran into Cathi-Ann, who was speechless in her surprise at running into Lorelei. To ease the other girl's discomfort, Lorelei said, "It must be my day to run into people; I just saw Mei Lundgren at the art supply store."

"Oh! Lore! Um, hi!" exclaimed Cathi-Ann, rather loudly. This was followed by a pause, which hung awkwardly between them until she continued, "Look, I'm sorry. I'm not a very good friend. I just can't handle serious stuff, not that I haven't thought about you a lot…"

"It's okay, Cathi-Ann. I admit, I was hurt and angry for a bit, but not any more. Everything's fine, now. I've never been happier."

Her outspoken friend blinked in surprise, then said, "Oh, well, good. You wanna have a drink some time and tell me all about it? Not 'there' but somewhere nice?"

Recognizing the invitation was by way of apology, Lorelei laughed and said, "Yes, of course." The truth was that Lorelei felt she owed Cathi-Ann an explanation, as she did not know about the cancer. Cathi-Ann was one of the few people who could make her laugh out loud, and she did enjoy her company, and it was obvious Cathi-Ann enjoyed hers as well. Lorelei accepted that it was part of Cathi-Ann's character to run from tragedy just as Paula had dedicated her life to soothing pain caused by it. Kwok Lee had taught her that there were many levels of relationship.

Though his feelings for her were evident in his attentiveness to her, he had not yet even kissed her. In insecure moments she wondered if he was having second thoughts about her, but she could not question him. Lorelei was fully recovered, her libido was a constant reminder of that; she often felt she would boil over with the heat of her attraction for Kwok Lee when he was nearby. Lorelei wondered if it was the same for him; sometimes she caught him looking at her in a way that made her believe that soon, the day would dawn when they would come together as one.

She threw herself into her artwork, and as October came to an end, her days fell into a happy pattern of working to produce pieces for the gallery by day, and contented companionship with Kwok Lee in the evenings. At the end of a day that had been so busy for both of them that she had not seen Kwok Lee all day despite being mere footsteps away from him, Lorelei quietly approached him as he finished tallying the day's takings in the back room of the shop.

"I've finished the big serigraph. Come and see." He followed her into the studio, to the drying rack in the corner where the prints would sit until the ink was entirely dry. One of the large, six-colour prints lay on the top of the rack. It depicted a small, light-coloured dog seen from an oblique angle, its shadow a dark diagonal smudge across the bottom of the work. The background consisted of winter-brown leaves and twigs, with green shoots poking through the dead vegetation. She held her breath as Kwok Lee studied the print, wondering if he appreciated how much work went into a six-colour serigraph. He looked at her, slate-blue eyes wide with wonder.

"It's you, Lorelei. I mean where you are right now. The dog's shadow is very sharp, and dark, like fear, and the dead leaves are what you are leaving behind; new life is springing from them. The dog is life, though there is fear in its eyes, it is looking forward."

As he finished speaking, Lorelei's green eyes reflected his wonder. "Yes! But it was totally unconscious on my part..."

"The best art often is," he replied. "Are you ready to stop for dinner, or do you want to continue working?"

"Doesn't matter; either way is fine. What did you want to do?"

"I'm not hungry right now; I think I'll go up and have a cup of tea and rest awhile."

"I'll stay down here, then. I have some monoprints I want to start on. I'll do that for a bit, then I'll come upstairs."

"Right, but don't make it too long, okay?"

She listened as he went up the stairs to the apartment above. She sighed; he was still looking after her, still making sure she did not overtax herself, though he agreed that she seemed to be fully cured, and seemed pleased that she was following a healthy and productive lifestyle. Though she had initially rebelled against the vegetarian diet he had prescribed, she had come to realize that she had never felt more alert, so she had elected to stay on the diet. She did not meditate as he did; instead she took long, solitary walks during which she often had the sense that she was watching herself from a vantage point high above her, which helped to make her feel very centred, and sure of the direction her life was taking.

Almost two hours later, Lorelei sat back and looked at her work. She had been labouring over her compositions; a monoprint plate being a surface to which things such as string, found objects, and the like were glued, then ink applied before the print was taken through the press. Being that the plates were very fragile, only one print could be taken from each plate.

She stretched and looked out the window. The sun had set on a beautiful early fall evening, and lights were beginning to come on in the surrounding buildings. Remembering that Kwok Lee had said not to take too long, she put away her projects, leaving the printing until tomorrow. He probably had a meal on the stove by now, as he did most of the cooking. As she climbed the stairs to the apartment, she caught the sweet smell of sandalwood. Incense must be burning; perhaps Kwok Lee was meditating.

Opening the door, Lorelei was amazed to find that there was no light in the apartment, except for strategically-placed groups of burning candles. The stereo was playing traditional Chinese violin music that was almost vocal in its haunting, yearning strains.

"Kwok Lee?" she called, walking toward the bedroom.

"Yes?" he answered. Something in his voice made her stop in her tracks as every fibre of her being became instantly alert. The door to the bedroom opened, revealing Kwok Lee, clad only in a floor-length deep red silk robe embroidered with a pattern of black double happy symbols and gold dragons. For a moment, they simply stood looking at each other. He was so handsome, with his thick, wavy hair framing his smooth face with its high cheekbones and piercing slate-blue eyes, that Lorelei, for just an instant, believed that she could be happy the rest of her life if she could just look at him.

Afterwards, she couldn't recall moving into his arms, she could only remember the feeling of ecstasy as she realized that tonight they would give in to their long-suppressed passion for each other. Though he held her close, he did not kiss her right away. He tipped her face up with one hand, while pulling her closer with the other.

"I'm sorry," he said, his voice hoarse with emotion.

"Sorry?" she said, nearly fainting in her desire for him.

"For making you wait, I had to be sure…sure that it was right…"

Desire made her bold. "Just kiss me!" she ordered.

He complied, smiling a little as he began to kiss her, a long, slow kiss that held the promise of many tomorrows. She was no longer Lorelei McMillan, art girl from Australia; she was a captured princess on board an Asian pirate's junk boat, destined for his seraglio. She sighed as the kiss ended; he buried his face in her hair as he murmured, "Lorelei, my Lorelei."

She leaned into him, revelling in the clean, masculine scent of him, and jumped a little when she could feel his enlarged manhood pressing against her abdomen. "Ohh, Kwok Lee, I want…I want…" she could say no more as he swept her up in his arms and took her to his bed. Swift fingers made short work of removing her clothing; he stood back gazing at her as she lay on the cobalt-blue silk sheets, her lovely red hair spilling out around her, the room ablaze with candlelight. Through heavy-lidded eyes, she regarded him with desire that was at least the equal of his; she trembled with anticipation as she saw how very well-endowed he was, and how smooth his bronzed skin appeared. How she disliked hairy men! Unconsciously, she licked her full lips, and at that, Kwok Lee slid onto the bed beside her and began kissing her neck while caressing her body. When he shifted position, she felt the heat of her desire intensify as he took the tip of one pink-tipped breast in his mouth. She trembled again as she felt his hand caress her inner thigh, quaked with delight as curious fingers slipped into her. His low laugh brought her temporarily out of her reverie.

"What?" she murmured, allowing her own fingers to gently caress his smooth, muscular body, delighted in the quiver of his response.

"Mmmm, you are very ready, aren't you?" he whispered.

"And you aren't? You should be in pain by now," she gently retorted.

"I am, the most beautiful pain I've ever experienced. And you, my sweet, can do with me what you will."

"Mmm, if you insist," she said, as she pushed him on to his back and straddled his abdomen. Placing her hands on either side of his head, she leaned over and whispered, "But not until you say the magic words."

His eyes flew open in surprise. "Words? I...I...oh...I love you!"

"That's better," she said, sitting up, and moving into position over his engorged member. She reached back and gently took his organ of love in her hand; she smiled as she heard Kwok Lee's sharp intake of breath as she did so. Slowly she lowered her weight upon him as he arched his back in response. She moaned softly as she shifted position slightly as he was so large it hurt when the full length of him penetrated her. Instinct took over as she began to move slowly up and down on top of him; she leaned over, the tips of her breasts brushing his chest, as he began to rock his hips against her; looking into his eyes, she saw reflected there his passion, his desire, and his love for her. She sat up again, riding him as if he was a stallion galloping across the Mongolian plains, free and wild in timeless abandon. Little involuntary cries of ecstasy escaped her as waves of delight began to wash over her; as he shuddered to his own rapturous joy, she cried out in exultation. *She* had been the one he had waited for! *She* had ended his long solo journey! And she loved him! Yes, she loved him!

Finally satiated, she leaned forward and rested her weight on his chest as he wrapped his arms around her.

"Easy," he whispered. "I'm still inside you…"

As she slid off him, the evidence of his passion came spilling out of her.

"Yes, lots of you is still inside me," she said, snuggling against him.

"Get used to it," he said, stroking her hip.

"Promise?"

"Absolutely. Much more to come… especially on the honeymoon."

"H… honeymoon?" she gasped.

"Well, yes. I thought we could be wed here, and then go to Australia… maybe have a second wedding in Hong Kong. That is… if you want to marry me."

"Yes! Yes! Of course I do! Oh… Kwok Lee… I'm so happy… I love you…" she dissolved into tears as he cuddled her closer.

Kissing her forehead, he said, "And I promise to love you forever and always… now that we are healed."